Molly Greyson's Ghost

by
Roberta Hoffer

Young Adult Novel from
Dragonfly Publishing, Inc.

* * * * *

MOLLY GREYSON'S GHOST
Young Adult / Ghost Stories

Hardback Edition
EAN 978-1-941278-67-3
ISBN 1-941278-67-1

Paperback Edition
EAN 978-1-941278-68-0
ISBN 1-941278-68-X

eBook Edition
EAN 978-1-941278-69-7
ISBN 1-941278-69-8

Story Text ©2016 Roberta Hoffer
Cover Art & Illustrations ©2016 Terri Branson
Dragonfly Logo ©2001 Terri Branson

Published in the United States of America by
Dragonfly Publishing, Inc.
Website: www.dragonflypubs.com

* * * * *

CONTENTS

* * * * *

Acknowledgements

I could write an entire chapter of who I would like to acknowledge such as my family, close friends, and even co-workers. Many of the characters in this book are based on real people in my life. I love to observe people then use their quirks, personality traits, and mannerisms to fill out my characters. But the one who deserves the full amount of acknowledgement is My God and Savior, Jesus Christ. Without His guidance and strength I could not have accomplished writing yet another book. He has given me the wisdom, determination, and courage to put words together on a page to captivate the reader while still maintaining my Christian values. All glory goes to my Lord with prayers of hope for the continued ability to write future books for those who love to be entertained reading quality stories with happy endings.

∗ ∗ ∗ ∗

Dedication

I would like to dedicate this book to my Daughter-in-law, Erin. I have known her since she was sixteen years old. She has been somewhat of an inspiration in creating my main character for this book. From our first meeting to now she has matured and grown into a wonderful woman. She is not only my Daughter-in-law but a very loyal and good friend. My son made a wise decision when he married this lady. May their life together be filled with happy endings.

* * * * *

CHAPTER 1

TO avoid any sort of human communication, I sat in the rear of this monstrosity of a vehicle.

I was pouting, but for a very good reason.

My dad's company had transferred him to their newest high-tech architectural facility and promoted him to President.

Great for him. Great for Mom. Not so great for me.

This new job just happened to be located in the Midwest and in Indiana of all places.

Why would anyone *want* to move from beautiful sunny California to a dreary little state in the middle of the country? Not me. But that was exactly what happened without so much as any consideration to my feelings.

From what my computer told me, Indiana was flat and boring. That meant no beaches and certainly no surfer boys to ogle. Marvelous. I had been uprooted from the only home I had known and moved three quarters of the way across the country, leaving a thriving metropolis with sandy white beaches to live in a little town with nothing but cornfields as far as the eye could see. I was getting ready to start my junior year of high school. I had friends that I had been in school with since first grade. Not to mention my gorgeous boyfriend, Dylan. How could I expect to keep a long distance relationship going until I was eighteen and able to make my own decisions? I was quite certain there were numerous girls just waiting in line to jump at the chance to take my place. All this seemed like child abuse to me.

And how could it get any worse? Well, for one, Dad opted to pass on the complimentary airline tickets and drive this monster the two thousand plus miles to our destination. Not that I wanted to get to Indiana any sooner. He said it would be an opportunity for us to 'see this great country of ours up close and personal'. He also said our house wouldn't be ready for at least a week, so we could take our time. Kind of like a mini-vacation. Yippee. It was hard to see anything burrowed down in the back seat with a phone glued to my face.

One of the many perks of this promotion, I was told, was this vehicle. I preferred to call it the *tank*. Technically, it was a SUV, sport utility vehicle. I wasn't certain why we had to have something so huge to get us around Indiana, unless we needed extra protection from the country folk. As much as I detested this vehicle and the length of the trip, I had to admit there were some positive attributes to it. It had built in Wi-Fi, picking up signals from cell towers as we traveled, and a charging port in the armrest of my seat. At least, I kept in constant touch with my now abandoned California friends. They sent pictures of the picnic they had on the beach. Without me. I sent pictures of the backseat of the SUV.

Our first required stop was Las Vegas.

"Come on, Molly," Mom said, as she opened my door.

The scorching hot pavement tossed wavy images onto the side of the gigantic hotel looming before me.

"I'm fine right here." I reached for the door to close it, only to find my dad's hand with a firm grip on the handle.

"Get out of the car and stop pouting," Dad commanded. "Las Vegas is a beautiful place and you're going to enjoy it."

Seemed like lately he was telling me how I felt even though he didn't have a clue about my true feelings.

I wanted to turn around and head west. Instead I was being dragged into a twenty story hotel with fancy fountains and a lobby decorated in gaudy purple velvet and gold tassels. While my parents stood in line to check us in, I flopped down in one of the lobby chairs and let all that purple surround me. Every few minutes I looked up from my phone to see what progress my parents had made. Still in line. For such a fancy place, they certainly were slow.

Bored, I leaned close to the large glass window. I pressed my face against it to get a better view of the 'strip', as tourists referred to it. The hotels went on and on in a never-ending offering of bigger and better attractions. Then I noticed an odd looking video game on the sidewalk.

I slipped out of the hotel and went to check it out. It wasn't a video game. At least none I had ever seen. There was a puppet-like female mannequin encased inside a three sided glass window box. It was life-sized and very strange looking, almost mesmerizing. The paint was beginning to peel away in places from the enchanting face and she was missing the little finger on her right hand. Her clothes were faded and worn, as if she had been in that box for decades without so much as an occasional dusting. She looked like a Gypsy, or at least how I imagined one might look. A dull multi-colored print bandana was tied around her black curly hair. Her clothing must have been very colorful once, but her face was like porcelain. Now she stood in front of a popular hotel in a popular city looking like all the rest of the homeless humans I had seen. Ignored and tossed aside.

Not this time. I was going to bring this mechanical marvel to life.

I searched for a switch to put the grand lady into motion. On the side was a slot with instructions to insert only dollar bills. What had happened to twenty-five cent machines?

I fished through my purse finding two one dollar bills. I inserted the first one and waited. Nothing. Had I just been conned out of one of my two dollars by a machine right here on Las Vegas Boulevard?

Just as I was about to walk away, the lifeless figure moved. Slowly at first, as if she had to gain momentum. Her head jerked from side to side in awkward movements. As her face came directly in line with mine, her eyes popped open, revealing deep black pools.

I jumped back, startled.

Then she froze. What? That's it?

I frantically stuffed my second dollar bill in the slot and waited. Not able to take my eyes from her face, her puppet mouth began to move. I took a step forward and leaned close, straining to hear her words. But all I heard were gears going into motion in a regimented sequence. Then a card popped out of a small opening in the front of the machine and fell to the pavement at my feet.

I picked up the card and read the words in silence: *Your journey will end where the once living still tread. Steer clear of the visions in the darkness for they are the ghosts of lost souls. Beware Molly Greyson, beware of.*

I dropped the card like it was a piece of hot coals and looked up at the porcelain face.

Her eyes slammed shut and her head dropped to her chest motionless.

I backed away and accidentally bumped into a man, causing him to drop his luggage and briefcase. Papers flew into the air, littering the sidewalk and sticking to the puddles left from an earlier passing rain. My card was lost in an ocean of endless paper. I apologized and tried to help gather the papers. He grumbled something under his breath and stuffed the unorganized dirty papers back into his briefcase and stalked away.

I scanned the sidewalk for the card. Then I spied it a few feet away in the gutter. It floated on a gentle stream of dirty street water and who knows what else mixed in. I raced through the crowd of sightseers, like a salmon swimming upstream. I dove down and snatched the card right before the murky water poured into a sewer grate and out of my reach forever.

I returned to the now frozen statue inside the case and stared at it. Had I imagined it? How had the machine known my name? I knew now that her lips had been mouthing the words on the card. She had said 'beware'. Visions, ghosts, and lost souls. What was she trying to warn me about? We were going to a little town in Indiana. Probably a boring little town that would be lucky to have any excitement at all, much less ghosts. Not that the idea of ghosts didn't get my attention. I was really into reading about ghosts and the paranormal, but this had to be a bunch of nonsense, just a way to get me to put more money in the slot to get her to talk again. It was a Las Vegas gimmick, plain and simple.

Out of dollar bills and out of patience with this mechanical hoax, I popped the card in my jeans pocket.

Through the hotel's front glass I could see Mom and Dad standing at the registration desk, speaking with the hotel staff and oblivious that I had even wandered off. Before I walked inside the lobby, I turned and gave a quick glance toward the Gypsy-in-a-box.

I stopped cold. Her head was turned toward me, and she was smiling in a way that was not puppet-like at all.

I raced into the lobby and didn't look back. The rest of the time we spent in Las Vegas I made a mental point to avoid the mystical box, never looking even remotely in her direction.

* * *

"RISE and shine, Sleepyhead," my dad announced, yanking the covers off me. "It's a beautiful day and next stop is the Grand Canyon."

Whoopee, I thought, reaching for the covers. Hadn't the night before been ripe with enough family togetherness? The room filled with blinding light. I covered my face with my hands and peeked through my fingers to see what had caused such pain to my still sleepy eyes. Dad had pulled open the room darkening blinds and stood at the foot of my bed, grinning from ear-to-ear. I knew the option of returning back to bed wasn't up for debate. But waking up and realizing that we were still on our way to Indiana was reality turned into a bad dream.

I pulled myself out of bed and struggled to get my bags together.

We were leaving behind the crowded glitzy casinos and heading for what I was certain was a wide open hole in the earth. Thoughts of mechanical gypsies and threats of ghosts filled my head. I reached into my jeans pocket and felt the card still secure where I had placed it. I had convinced myself that I was delusional due to the stress of the move and the heat of the Nevada desert.

As we drove out of the hotel parking garage, I stole a glance toward the front of the hotel where the Gypsy-in-a-box had stood. Gone. She was gone.

Was that good or bad? Well, it didn't matter now. We were leaving her and Las Vegas behind. Good riddance!

Through my backseat tank window, I watched as the hotels faded into the distance.

"Sorry people, but we need gas," Dad said, as he pulled into a gas station. "This baby seems to be awfully thirsty."

Great, now Dad was referring to this hunk of metal as his 'baby'. Disgusting.

"I'm going to get something to drink," Mom said, as she looked over the seat toward me. "Want anything?"

I didn't answer. I just opened my door and decided to go in and pick out what I wanted. If I let Mom pick it out she would bring me one of those protein waters. I just wanted a smoothie like I got in California. I doubted this gas station had smoothies. I was right. I settled for a frozen orange drink.

As I rounded the corner to the checkout counter, I came face to face with the Gypsy fortune teller, who now stood by the exit door.

I was so stunned my drink dropped from my hand making a huge splash as it hit the floor. Candy bars and snack crackers were covered in frozen orange drink.

The Gypsy's mouth was open wide as if she was laughing, but her eyes were dark and eerie. I was frozen to the spot. I studied her carefully. Indeed, she was the very same Gypsy on which I had squandered my dollar bills. How could this be?

"Molly, are you alright?" Mom asked.

"I'm—I'm fine," I stuttered.

How had this machine turned up at the very gas station where my dad chose to stop?

"I'm so sorry for the mess," Mom said to the store clerk. "Can I help clean it up?"

The clerk shook his head in refusal. He handed Mom a replacement for my drink. Then we stepped around the mess on the floor.

Other customers were staring at me. I felt my face heat up and was sure I had turned beet red. I just wanted to get out of there, but that meant walking past the Gypsy.

With my head lowered, I headed past the box. Then a strong urge came over me. Unable to resist, I lifted my head and faced the magical machine. Her mouth formed a word. I raced through the door but not before I heard her voice this time: *Beware.*

Climbing into the tank, I buried myself in my little corner of the back seat and sucked down the frozen orange drink so fast my head began to throb. Great. Brain freeze.

Feeling like I was losing control, I punched in Robyn's cell-phone number. The call went straight to voice mail. Great. I tried Dylan and got his voice mail, too.

I tried to come up with a good explanation of how I had come into contact again with that machine. Nothing seemed to make any sense.

I closed my eyes as the SUV purred along the desert highway. Sleepy and mentally exhausted, I drifted off, hoping to wake to the warmth of a California sun reassuring me this was all just a bad dream.

CHAPTER 2

THE sound of an oldies song on the car radio woke me from a much needed nap.

Mom and Dad were singing, if you could call it that.

Now that I was awake I decided to try Dylan again. I pressed his name in my contacts favorites and waited with excited anticipation as the phone began to ring. I had not been able to reach him but once in the three days we had been gone. Come to think of it, everyone I tried to call recently went directly to voice mail. What was up with that? I missed Dylan so very much. I really needed to hear his voice. Just before voice mail clicked on so I could leave yet another message, a girl's voice answered. She sounded out of breath.

"Yes?" she said in a voice like an angel choir.

Stunned, I hesitated for a moment. "Who's this?" I asked.

"Who's this?" the angelic voice questioned back.

"This is Molly, Dylan's girlfriend," I replied a little defensively. "And who are you?"

There was a moment of hesitation on her end. "There must be some mistake," she replied. "I don't know any Molly. I'm Melissa, and I'm Dylan's—"

"Molly?" Dylan said with heavy breaths. "Where are you? How is the trip? Are you in Indiana yet?"

"Who is Melissa?" I demanded.

"W-w-what?" Dylan stuttered. "Oh, um, just a friend."

"Just a friend?" Melissa shouted in the background, her angelic voice turned shrill with jealousy. "Tell her who I am or I will!"

"No need, I get the picture, Dylan," I said choking back the tears. "I've only been gone three days. Obviously, absence does not make the heart grow fonder."

Click.

I slammed my phone on the floor of this rolling prison and buried my face in a travel pillow to muffle the sounds of crying. I was heart-broken. How could Dylan do this to me? And so quickly. Unless he already had *her* waiting in the wings. I thought we had agreed to keep this relationship going, even though I was moving two thousand miles away. I had planned to talk to him every day on my trip. Then when I got settled into my new room, we would be able to face-talk every day through the phone or the computer. I was glad the video had not been on, because I sure did not want to see that Melissa creature.

I sat up, wiped the tears from my face, and pulled my long auburn hair out of my eyes. I may not have been a blonde beach bunny, but I had green eyes and a light sprinkling of freckles. I had my dignity. Where I was going there wouldn't be any girls running around in string bikinis to lure away boyfriends. There were no beaches or cabanas or sand volleyball courts. I should fit right in with my fair skin that freckled when I got too much California sun and my dark hair that contrasted sharply with the white sun-bleached blondes of Southern California. Maybe Indiana wouldn't be so terrible after all.

Oh, who was I kidding? I was trying to psych myself up to live in a place I was sure had nothing interesting. Nothing I was used to. And no Dylan.

Well, that was a moot point now, since there was obviously no Dylan for me in California. Would there be a Dylan for me in Indiana? No, that was too much for hope for.

I hugged my travel pillow to my chest and buried my face once again as the tears returned. I wasn't ready to accept Dylan's betrayal, and I certainly wasn't ready to lay down roots in some forsaken Midwest town with anyone else.

* * *

THE Grand Canyon was just what I had expected. It was an enormous hole in the earth cut through the desolate dry west with a river as its knife.

I compared it to my heart, as I stared into the vastness. Both were deep and empty with a small trickle of hope at the very bottom. My old high school literature teacher would love that analogy. It might even have gotten me an A+.

Much to my chagrin, I had to admit that the canyon was awesome at sunset. It actually gave the sunset off the ocean at West Beach a run for its money. Except everything here felt real and up close. Maybe I was starting to see things from a different perspective. Maybe what I lived in for so long had been a forerunner to reality. I had heard people refer to Californians as "plastic people." Had I become one of the "plastic people" without realizing it? Was this trip opening my eyes to what the rest of the world offered?

As the tank rolled eastward, leaving behind the beauty of the Grand Canyon, I thought about Indiana. I had no idea what to expect. I had never been outside of California except for a trip to Hawaii, and that had been a far cry from Indiana. Of that I was certain. My stomach lurched when I tried to imagine my new school. There were more students enrolled in my old high school alone than the total population of the city to which we were moving. Quaint. I'd have to make new friends. Or not. I wasn't one of the most outgoing people. It was a no-brainer that my 'friends' from California had moved on, or had already forgotten me. *Plastic friends.* That seemed quite apparent, since Robyn had never answered my messages and Dylan had a new—well, had moved on. Maybe it was time for *me* to move on. I wasn't going to be one of those plastic people anymore.

I pulled out of a depressed slump and looked out the window. The great Rocky Mountains loomed before me, snow capping the tallest peaks. I had seen snow only once before when we went snowboarding in Northern California. That had been easy for me, since I had been practically raised on a surf board. Same principle. Different kind of surf. It occurred to me that Indiana had snow in the winter. Maybe I could get in some snowboarding. Maybe not though, since snowboarding required mountains. I was pretty sure Indiana didn't have any of those.

We spent the next two days visiting mines and hiking in the mountains. Family togetherness was not so horrible, but I wasn't going to admit that. With much begging I convinced Mom and Dad to swing by Keystone. A few tenacious mounds of Colorado winter snow still dotted the mountainside there. Although the ski runs were not open, I was thrilled to find some of the main gondolas running.

As I sat in the back seat, sipping a mango smoothie, I watched the mountains that rolled from one peak to the next, like a river flowing with pointed waves.

* * *

THE highway stretched out through the flatness of Kansas, leaving the Rockies behind me.

I watched as fields bursting with millions of sunflowers went on and on for miles. They turned their heads following the sun as it crossed the plains. I vowed to return one day to the great mountains. I never dreamed that I could enjoy anything as much as the ocean as its waves pushed and pulled on a lazy sunny day. But the overwhelming majesty of the mountains had captured my heart. Visions of knee-deep snow filled my head. I wondered if anything in Indiana would change my mind as profoundly about California. I doubted it.

Wow! Could my dad be right? He told Mom and me all along that this little cross country trip would be good for all of us. It would give us a chance to allow our heads to accept the move. If we had flown, we would have been in California in the morning and in Indiana in the afternoon. Talk about a shock to the system. Maybe Dad had been right.

Oh no! That was how adults thought. I had just turned sixteen. I should be thinking about parties and boys and new shoes. Was this trip making me old before my time?

I turned up the volume on my earbuds and settled into a more comfortable position in my temporary rolling apartment. I saw Dad's face in the rearview mirror.

"Hey, girl," Dad shouted above the music blaring in my ears. "I'll wake you when we get to St. Louis. I wouldn't want you to miss the arch."

I forced a gracious smile and nodded to the face in the rearview mirror. Dad was really trying to make this an eventful trip, hoping to ease the pain he had brought into my life. No teenager wanted to be uprooted and replanted in a strange land. My thoughts wandered as the music changed from head-banging guitars to a softer more mellow tone.

What about Mom? I really hadn't considered her feelings about this move. She seemed to accept it. She was married to Dad, so she went where he went. I had been holding a personal pity-party and never thought to ask her how she felt about the move. What a great daughter I was. Mom might have had her own reservations about this drastic change to all of our lives, but she had never said a negative thing to me about it. That was strength.

Wait. Were those more adult thoughts creeping into my brain?

I tried to get some sleep, but my mind was in overdrive. I felt like a different person.

Maybe Indiana wouldn't be so terrible, after all.

CHAPTER 3

CONSIDERING the confining seatbelt, I shifted to my side as best as I could and saw something white on the floor.

I reached down and picked it up. It was the card from the Gypsy. I had managed to put the Gypsy out of my mind for a while. Now that card stared at me, renewing both fear and curiosity.

I read the card in silence. *Your journey will end where the once living still tread. Steer clear of the visions in the darkness for they are the ghosts of lost souls. Beware Molly Greyson, beware of.*

I had been stressing over the new school, new friends, and a new life style, but I had not allowed myself to stress over words on a card that had shot out of a dilapidated glass box. Now those words consumed me. My journey must have meant this trip. It would end in Indiana. But the *once living tread* lost me. No, if I connect that to the next words, *ghosts of lost souls*, then it must mean ghosts. That is, if I believed in that sort of thing. I wasn't all that certain I did.

I returned the card to my jeans pocket and readjusted my sleep position for the rest of the trip, not allowing myself to dwell on the possibilities that lay ahead.

A hand on my shoulder startled me awake. I jumped, swinging my arms as though swatting something out of my face.

"Hey, careful there, young lady," Dad said, as I opened my eyes to see his face. "You must have had a whale of a nightmare. You've been moaning and flip-flopping for the last one hundred miles."

I rubbed my eyes and stepped out of the tank. We were in the parking lot of the famed St. Louis Arch. I stared up into the sunny sky as the reflection on the silver arch flashed, nearly blinding my still sleep-filled eyes. I covered my face and turned toward the SUV, hoping to return to the semi-darkness offered by the tinted windows.

"Not so fast," Dad said, as he gently grabbed my shoulders and steered me in the opposite direction. "We're going up in the arch."

"Yea," I muttered.

"I heard that, Molly," Dad said. "This is our last stop before we get to Indiana. This is exciting."

Shutting the door behind me, I decided to make my dad's day and go up in the arch with him. Mom gave me the 'thank you' look. I had the feeling she wasn't as excited as Dad was. She didn't particularly like heights. Well, if she could do this for Dad and overcome her fears, then I'd pretend to enjoy the arch, too.

Going up in a curved structure was not possible in your average up and down elevator. The one here was an odd little compartment that was less than appealing. Once inside the small egg-shaped elevator, I found a new type of fear. Claustrophobia set in and I felt trapped inside the egg. The strange little elevator creaked and groaned as it jerked its way up. I couldn't wait to get to the top and out of the weird little compartment.

Mom's face had turned a pale shade of green. She gripped the arm rest so tightly that her fingernails were starting to turn blue.

When the egg stopped and the door opened, I flew out as if shot out of a cannon. I stopped short of the massive window that hung over the city of St. Louis as the mighty Mississippi River flowed beneath us. A queasy feeling filled my stomach, and I searched for the restroom sign. Spying the sign, I made my way through the crowd.

Mom was close on my heels. We both stood over the sinks splashing water on our faces. Together we gripped the sinks with our hands to steady ourselves as we looked over at each other with knowing smiles. I could tell that Mom was just as nauseated as I was. We returned to find Dad practically lying on the slanted windows to get a better view.

"Girls, come here," Dad said, his gaze riveted on the scenery far below. "Look at the muddy Mississippi down there. Isn't it amazing?"

"Thanks, dear, but I think we'll pass," Mom said, thankfully excusing both of us. "We'll wait for you by the elevator."

Oh no, I hadn't taken into consideration I would have to return to the ground in the same little egg. Sweat beads formed on my forehead. I searched the area for an exit sign that would offer me another alternative to return to the ground below. Stairs? Not likely. The doors slid open. Mom and I looked at each other. Dad pushed us inside. I closed my eyes, trying to ignore the elevator's peculiar jerks. Finally the egg stopped, and Mom and I quickly abandoned Dad.

"Wasn't that amazing?" Dad asked. "Did you get lots of pictures?"

My phone never left my pocket. Grabbing a can of lemon lime soda, I climbed back into the tank.

Only four more excruciating hours, and we would be in Indiana.

CHAPTER 4

TOTALLY wiped out, I had not opened my eyes since we left St. Louis.

I felt the tank stop and heard the sound of slamming doors.

Rolling down the window, I squinted at the scene before me. The air smelled fresh, not filled with gas emissions. The sun peaked in and out behind a row of tall oak trees that lined the driveway where we had stopped. Mom and Dad stood a short distance away, talking to a man.

This must be Indiana.

The man was dressed in casual khakis with a light blue dress shirt. He looked like he could have lived in California. It's not like I expected Indiana townsfolk to be dressed in bib overalls and checked shirts. Okay, well, maybe a little. I strained to hear what they were discussing.

"Really?" Dad questioned the man. "The house won't be ready until Tuesday? But I put my top notch guys on this project. They assured me it would be ready by today."

Great, now we had to find a place to stay for two more days. I wandered out in hopes of eavesdropping on the conversation.

Dad saw me coming and waved me toward him. "John, this is our daughter Molly."

"John is the realtor who found this magnificent house for us Molly," Dad said to me as I nodded to the man.

"I think you're going to like it here Molly," John said. "There are a lot of nice kids in this town."

I nodded again and then looked for the house. We stood just inside huge iron gates that seemed to be an entrance for a blacktop driveway. But I didn't see a house. The gates were massive, looming above us at least ten feet tall. They were made out of black cast iron with a unique design running through them. It looked like small animals, possibly dogs. Looking closer I realized they were dogs with wings, ferocious looking with barred teeth. They were gargoyles. This seemed a bit freaky to me, but I figured Dad loved it. He was all about the character of the houses he designed. Although this wasn't one of his designs, I could see by the way he was admiring the gates that he approved of it.

"Why don't you drive up to the house before you go into town?"

John asked. "At least you will get to see the amazing estate and the exquisite work that has already been completed."

"Everyone in the car," Dad said with excitement. "Let's go check out our new home. I'm anxious to see how the renovations are going."

I looked over at Mom, who seemed as depressed as I was. What was with this place? Dad had never been this excited over a house. He acted like it was going to be some sort of magical castle.

We all hopped back into the tank. My curiosity was peaked. I left my window down to get a better view of the long and winding driveway. Trees lined each side and reminded me of the southern plantations I had seen in my history books. The air smelled of fresh mown grass with an unknown sweet scent mixed with it. The effect was almost intoxicating.

Then I saw it. The trees gave way to a circular drive, placing us directly in front of a monstrous house. It looked old but somehow new. It was probably the newly installed landscaping that helped hide the aging building. The house sported a curious blend of stone and bricks. A porch wrapped around it, like a cozy shawl. The house had two—no, three stories, and a garage was attached by a bridge like structure.

Jumping out of the SUV, I looked up and tried to take in the massiveness of our new home. My eyes fixed on a cylindrical protrusion on one end of the house that went from the ground to the third level. It was as if a grain silo had been placed on the side of it. It had two round windows and one long window between them just below a fancy roof. It reminded me of a castle.

"The house has new shake shingles," John explained. "As requested, they sand blasted the exterior. The interior has been updated. The wood floors have been restored to their original beauty. I cannot wait until you see the spiral oak staircase."

He sounded like he was trying to sell the house to us. I knew that Dad's company had purchased it for what Dad termed "a song," and all we had to do was agree to live here for five years. He had enlisted the top crew from the new company to do all the renovations. Dad always took pride in his projects, but he was treating this like it was his 'baby'. *Piece of cake* Dad had reassured his CEO. Well, in less than five years I would be out of here and at a nice college back in sunny California. At least, that was my plan.

"The house originally had eight bedrooms but no bathrooms," John reported.

I stopped dead in my tracks. "There are no bathrooms?" I blurted.

"Yes, of course there are bathrooms." John seemed a bit frustrated.

"As I was saying, there were eight bedrooms, but now there are only five. The other three have been converted into spacious bathrooms."

I let out a heavy sigh. John looked at me through squinted eyes as if to scold me. We followed John up the steps and onto the porch.

"Plenty of room for porch swings to lull away the hot summer nights," John rambled.

He sounded more like a commercial than a realtor. He unlocked the box hanging from the curved brass handle on the oversized oak and glass door. Then he stood back and allowed us to enter first.

"Exactly when was this house built?" Mom asked, stepping over the threshold.

All eyes turned to John.

"Well," he stammered, "I believe the deed said it was built in 1876."

"Excuse me?" Mom asked in that high-pitched tone that meant she was upset. "What year did you just say?"

"Um...1876," John repeated sheepishly.

"Well, that explains why there was no indoor plumbing," Dad said in his usual jovial voice. Pushing past Mom, he entered the house. He gave a low approving whistle, which echoed through the enormous entry hall.

Yes, I would say Dad was more than pleased with the work his crew had accomplished.

Mom and I looked at each other. I knew what she was thinking. What had Dad gotten us into? This place could rival Dracula's castle. The only things missing so far were the bats and ghouls.

I looked around at the empty hall. Dad saw the potential, but I had to strain a little harder to envision the finished product. Since the furniture wouldn't be arriving for another two days, the emptiness made the house seem that much larger. The massive grand staircase rose before us like a mountain, as it split into two directions at the second floor. I decided to check it out.

"Just a minute young lady!" Dad called to me. "Where do you think you're off to?"

"To check out the bedrooms," I replied. "And pick out mine now."

"I think you should wait for your mother and me to choose our bedroom first," Dad stated with authority.

"If I might make a suggestion," John interrupted. "I believe I know the perfect place for your bedroom, Molly."

I looked at John with surprise. How could he possibly know the perfect bedroom for me? He had just met me ten minutes ago. But then he knew this house better than I did. I decided to let him show me what he assumed was the *perfect bedroom* for me. As long as it had one of those spacious bathrooms he was talking about, I might agree.

"That's an excellent idea," Dad chimed in. "We'll all go upstairs and see what other surprises there are. You can show Molly what you had in mind for her."

Just great. I felt like I was in a boarding school and the headmaster was taking me to my assigned room while my parents visited.

I followed John with Mom and Dad close behind. Dad grinned, while Mom showed obvious signs of hesitation.

As we reached the second story landing, I expected to stop at one of the closed doors along the long hallway. We didn't stop. As we walked, John explained that these were all bedrooms, but he had a special one in mind for me. We continued on to the end of the hall, where another set of stairs lead up to the third floor. These stairs were narrow with ancient floral carpeting. The stairway was lit with wall sconces and that castle idea popped back into my head.

"These are the west wing stairs to the third floor," John explained. "They will take us to the ballroom. Then to the room I believe will be perfect for Molly's bedroom. I apologize for the outdated carpet. The crew was following instructions to leave some of the original touches to make the house unique. The east wing stairs are at the opposite end of this hall, where there are optional maid and butler quarters."

Did he mean there were rooms for a maid and a butler? That would be awesome. No more dishes or laundry to do.

I wasn't keen on the burgundy and gold carpet with flowers the size of dinner plates, but if Dad wanted to retain some originality I wasn't going to argue.

At the top of the stairs John turned left toward an oddly shaped door. It was rounded at the top but fit nicely into the framework that encased it.

"Your new bedroom, Miss Greyson," John said with a bow as if he were entertaining royalty.

I walked toward the curious door and opened it. As I entered the room, I knew immediately where I was. The room was almost round. I was in the cylindrical part of the house. I walked across the floor to the windows and looked out on the driveway and front lawn. The SUV tank didn't look as huge from up here.

"Well?" Dad asked. "Was John right? Is this the perfect bedroom for you?"

I turned around to face the three adults waiting for my decision.

"Yes," I replied. "I do believe this is the most perfect room for me."

I felt a smile cross my lips, perhaps the first since leaving California. Was I actually going to like it here? Could I be happy living in this monstrosity we would soon be calling home? What's happening to me?

"I had a feeling when I met you that this would be the ideal room for you," John said with obvious pride. He pointed to the other two doors in the room that were shaped like the entry door. "This door leads to the closet, and the other leads to the bathroom. I'm certain once you see them, you will be pleased."

"Well, John, since you did such a superb job of choosing Molly's bedroom, do you have a room in mind for us?" Dad asked.

"I think you will find any of the four bedrooms on the second floor pleasing," John replied, as he turned toward the stairs.

"There are no other bedrooms on the third floor?" Mom asked. "Molly will be up here by herself?"

I didn't see that as a problem. We were finally in a house big enough for me to play music and surf the web without the parents breathing down my neck.

"Maybe Mom is right, Molly," Dad said. "Being up here all alone might not be such a wise idea."

"No really, I'll be fine," I pleaded. "John was right. This is the ideal room for a teenager. Remember when you were a teenager, Dad? Didn't you want a little privacy way back then?"

Dad blinked. "Yes, of course, even with my fleeting memory I can remember what it was like to be a teenager."

"I didn't mean—"

"I know what you meant, Molly. If I were you I'd pick this room, too. How many kids get to sleep in a round room?" Dad gave me an approving hug and turned to Mom. "Let's go pick out our room."

As Mom walked away she glanced over her shoulder at me. It was an odd look. The wrinkles between her eyebrows creased deeply. It wasn't normal for my mom's beautiful face. It was almost as if she were worried.

Closing the door behind them, I looked around the empty circular room and envisioned where my furniture would go.

I rushed over to the bathroom door and opened it to find an enormous bathtub with legs that looked a lot like animal paws. It fit the house perfectly. I was definitely a shower-type girl, but the thought of a hot bubble bath in the deep tub had a lot of potential.

Then I wandered back through the bedroom and opened the closet door. The huge space was filled with shelves for shoes, lots of shoes, and racks for clothes. It was teenager-heaven.

Then I noticed something in the back of the dark closet. I felt for a light switch, but couldn't find one. Looking up, I spied a long cord hanging from the ceiling. I pulled the cord and the light above me came on. What I had seen in the darkness now looked like a roll of carpet. The workers had probably placed it in here to finish the closet.

Then I noticed it was covering what looked like a door only this door was considerably smaller than the closet door. I pushed the roll of carpet aside and it fell to the floor in a cloud of dust. From the musty smell I realized this wasn't new carpet but an old rug rolled up and stored in here from previous owners.

I reached for the round knob on the small door and tried to turn it. It didn't budge. Maybe it was just stuck. I pulled hard and then tried to push but it still wouldn't move. Under the knob was a small hole in the shape of what might be found on a treasure chest. I assumed it was for a key. I searched the empty closet but did not find a key.

I pulled the cord on the light and shut the door behind me. As I turned to leave, I thought I heard a faint voice coming from inside the closet. I opened the door quickly and pulled the cord, lighting the darkness of the closet. Nothing. I went to the small door and jiggled the knob. Still locked tight.

Shutting off the light, I closed the closet door once again. I stood completely still just outside and listened. Silence.

Certain my imagination was getting the better of me, I went to find my parents. It had been a long trip. I was tired and my mind must have been playing tricks on me.

I pulled my phone out of my jeans pocket to see if I had any bars this far out in the boonies. The Gypsy's card fell on the floor face up in front of me. A wave of unexpected chills ran up my spine, as if the words printed on the card had just screamed at me.

CHAPTER 5

PICKING up the card, I shoved it into back in my pocket and tried not to think about it.

I should have thrown it away, but something compelled me to hang on to it.

Voices echoed ahead of me. When I reached the double stained-glass doors, I could hear Mom. This time her tone was soft and happy.

I pushed open the doors and stepped into an enormous room. Three large glass chandeliers hung from the ceiling. The late afternoon sun shone through long windows. Light reflected off the cut crystal pieces, casting rainbows that danced across the room. The walls were filled with old photos in ornate gold frames. I walked around the room observing each one.

"The pictures are actual photos of galas the previous owners held here in this very ballroom," John explained.

Many of the photos were faded and yellow. The older photos were in black and white. Some had dates in the bottom right corner. In one photo ladies in long full dresses and impossibly small waists danced with men dressed in suits with long jackets and ruffled shirts. Some photos showed groups at parties. Most of the party guests were adults around the same age as my parents. One picture included a teenage girl with curly blonde hair. The adults in the photo with her seemed to be celebrating, but the girl looked distracted by something.

I leaned closer to get a better look at the girl. She had a pretty face. Her hair hung in tight curls down below her shoulders. Her dress looked like it was made of fancy printed satin with a row of lace framing her delicate white shoulders. But my attention was drawn to her eyes. She wasn't looking at the camera. Her eyes were focused to the right, wide open as if watching something intently.

"The pictures are quite interesting, aren't they?" John asked, as he walked up behind me.

I jumped at the sound of his voice. "Yes," I stammered. "But why are they still hanging on the walls? Did the previous owners know the people in the photos? Were they family members?"

"I'm not sure," John replied with a shrug. "Possibly to preserve the history of the house. This is the one room that has been left almost untouched since the original construction. The last owners weren't descendants of the Kotter family. When they moved out, they left suddenly without any explanation."

"Were any of the other owners' family members?" I queried. "And when was it the last non-family owners moved out exactly?"

John seemed frustrated with me. I didn't care, I wanted answers.

He began fidgeting with his briefcase. "I'm not certain of the exact date," he answered, "but it was only a couple of years ago that they left the estate in the hands of the bank." Sweat beads had begun to build on John's forehead, and he pulled nervously at the collar of his shirt.

What did John have to be nervous about? Was he hiding something?

"Well, whatever the reason, I think they are a nice touch to the ballroom," Mom chimed in, taking the pressure off John. "I think they should stay. I love the history here. I won't be changing it, either."

Mom gave me the 'that's enough, young lady' look, so I held the rest of my questions for another time.

I was surprised that Mom agreed to keep the photos. This room's yellowing flowered wallpaper and outdated chandeliers just didn't fit Mom's preference for sleek modern style. Yet I knew my friends from California would be green with envy over my round bedroom.

The sun hid behind a row of oak trees, as we walked out of the house. I turned and looked up at the round window, knowing that was my new bedroom. Maybe this wasn't going to be so awful after all.

"I have taken the liberty of booking two rooms at the Darby Lane Bed & Breakfast," John said. "Compliments of Indie Architects, Inc. per instructions from your CEO, Mr. Clemets, in Indianapolis."

I had never stayed in a bed and breakfast. It sounded pretty cool. I checked the bars on my phone. Still too low for service. Maybe once we got into town there would be better reception.

After climbing into the SUV, I plugged the phone into the Wi-Fi port and waited for a signal. I needed to talk to Robyn. Keeping in touch with her was the only remaining life-line to my old California life, now that Dylan had become a non-entity.

We sat in the driveway, while Dad got directions from John. I turned to take one more look at the place I was going to call home for the next chapter of my life. In the long middle window of my circular bedroom I thought I saw the figure of a person. I couldn't make out the face, but it looked like a female with blonde curly hair.

"Mom!" I shouted.

Mom turned around quickly. "What's wrong, Molly?"

The figure disappeared. I scanned the other windows. Nothing.

"I—um. Well, I thought I lost my phone. But I found it. Nothing to panic about. Sorry." I held up my phone and then slid down in my seat.

Was my mind playing tricks on me? I remembered thinking I had heard a voice coming from my closet. Now I thought I saw a figure in my bedroom window.

I must have watched too many scary movies. Girl moves to huge old house. Girl sees visions and hears voices. Girls meets ghost. Really? It was so very Hollywood, and I was not buying into it.

Ghosts were just the stuff of scary movies and hair-raising books. They were not real.

Right?

CHAPTER 6

WE passed one typical Midwest neighborhood after another.

Why couldn't our house be normal-looking instead of something straight out of Transylvania?

A sign along the road read: *Kottersville – Established 1886 – Population 5,435.* Would they change that to 5,438 to include our family?

As we drove down main street, we passed a fire station, a town hall, and a large brick building marked *Kottersville Police Station.* I counted three stop lights and two fast food restaurants. Well, at least I could get my favorite junk food. Hopefully, when I was able to inspect this place more thoroughly, I'd find some familiar stores scattered around. Surely I would be able to find a place to buy clothes and shoes. A girl could never have enough shoes.

We left behind the booming metropolis of Kottersville with its three big stop lights and headed back out into the countryside. It wasn't long before we pulled into the driveway of the inn with a quaint wooden sign that read: *Darby Lane Bed & Breakfast.*

Great. Another old house. Didn't they have any hotels?

We all piled out of the SUV ready for some food and a soft bed. The lady at the desk was friendly. Her hair was tied up in a messy bun, very acceptable and most modern. She had on a sundress and wore shiny gold sandals. This was more like it. Finally, something I could relate to.

"Good evening, Mr. and Mrs. Greyson," the lady said in a very pleasant voice. "My name is Emily Darby. My son and I are the owners of this establishment. Your room is ready. I also have a room for a Miss Molly Greyson."

I raised my hand like I was in school. Embarrassed, I grabbed my backpack and slipped behind Mom.

"My son, Dylan, will show you to your rooms," Mrs. Darby said.

Did she say Dylan? My heart jumped in my chest at the sound of the name. Dylan's face flashed through my brain and I envisioned him in his baggy swim trunks and wet blonde hair hanging over his deep blue eyes. I sighed. I knew this wasn't going to be my Dylan.

A tall boy came around the corner and held out his hand to Dad.

"Hello, I'm Dylan," he said in a very dreamy voice. "I'll help with your bags. Follow me."

As he reached down to pick up Mom's bag, he made eye contact with me. For a brief moment he froze.

"Dylan?" Mrs. Darby said. "The bags?"

Dylan looked away, focusing on the bags. I saw his muscles flex, as he lifted the bags with ease.

Oh, my.

Was I reading him wrong or had he just checked me out?

Well, this was promising.

Following along behind Mom and Dad, I took in every aspect of the guy walking ahead of us. Before we reached our rooms on the second floor, I had committed the details to memory. Dylan had shiny dark brown hair that hung past his shoulders and seemed to sway with every step he took. He was tall, probably six feet or better with a build that would rival any of the surfers I knew in California. I couldn't quite get a fix on his eyes, but I thought they were green. Yes, I was certain they were green. He wasn't tan like the boys back home, but he had a healthy look about him. It was no doubt he worked out with those arms.

Dylan unlocked the door and sat Mom's bag inside the room, holding the door for her very gentlemanly-like. Dad walked in after her and held out his hand with some bills in it.

"Thank you sir, but that's not necessary," Dylan said. He shook his hand instead of taking the money. He grabbed my bag and then turned to me. "Your room is just down the hall."

I could very well have carried my own bag, but I enjoyed watching his biceps flex as he toted it to my room for me.

Dylan unlocked my door and set my bag just inside, as he had done for Mom. After slipping through the doorway, I looked up into emerald green eyes. He held out his hand. I felt a wave of heat flush over my face, certain I must have turned a bright shade of crimson. I reached out and he took my hand with a firm grip, letting his fingers linger a bit longer than necessary.

In a moment, I pulled my hand from his and felt the tug of a smile.

"It was very nice to meet you, Molly Greyson," he said in that dreamy voice.

"Nice to meet you, too, Dylan Darby," I said, still locked in his liquid green stare.

He lowered his head and walked away.

So Indiana *did* have a Dylan. Maybe it wouldn't be so bad after all.

I shut the door behind me, closed my eyes, and slid down the back side of the door, becoming a teenage puddle of emotions on the floor. I tried to see California Dylan's face, but the only face popping up in my head was that of a tall dark-headed Indiana Dillon. I actually swooned out loud.

I opened my eyes to see a huge four-poster bed with a comforter filled with row after row of pink ruffles. There was actually a canopy over the bed with flowing pink ruffles to match. A dressing table with a large round mirror was to my right and a large cabinet with carved double doors stood on the left. I believe Mom had called them wardrobes, closets that were also furniture. This was definitely a girl's room. I was a girl, but not the ruffle-type. I was more California style geometric designs and bold colors, dressing like all the other girls my age and wearing the same hair style. Maybe it was time to be different. I ran my fingers over the ruffles, feeling very feminine. I turned and fell backwards, landing on the softness of the ruffles. I looked up at the canopy overhead and right then decided I wanted one of these in my new round room.

There was a knock on my door.

Rolling to my feet, I went to the door and opened it. There stood Mom and Dad.

"Are you getting ready?" they said together.

"Ready for what?" I asked.

"For dinner," Mom answered. "Mrs. Darby said supper would be served at six p.m. in the dining room. Here dinner is called supper."

"Oh, I guess I didn't hear her," I said, as my stomach let out a low growl.

"Maybe it was because you were so *fascinated* with her son," Mom said with a musical tone.

"Really, Mom?" I said with annoyance, and followed it up with a strategic snort. "I'll meet you downstairs at six."

But Mom was right. I had not taken my eyes off Indiana Dylan the entire time he had been with us. I pulled a sweater out of my bag and looked around for the bathroom. It had been a long ride, and I wanted to freshen up. I also wanted to make certain my hair was just right and my make-up wasn't a mess. Just in case.

There wasn't another door in the room. No bathroom? I went in search of a bathroom and found one two doors down. It must have been a community bathroom, since it wasn't connected to another room. I went in, and saw a large bathtub. No shower? Great. Then I remembered the clawfoot bathtub at my new house and decided to accept the change with dignity.

A quick look in the dimly lit mirror revealed messy hair plus a crease on my cheek from the nap I had taken earlier in the backseat of the tank.

Nice. Dylan must have thought I was a real slob.

I brushed my hair into a neat ponytail and tied it with a bow to match my peach sweater. I re-applied my blush and added a touch of lip gloss. Looking down at my phone, I saw it was five fifty-eight. Well, this would have to do. I didn't want to be late for 'supper'. I was starving.

I bounced down the stairs and met Mom and Dad in the lobby. When we entered the large dining room, there were already other people sitting at the long table. I assumed they were also guests. Mom nodded to another woman, and we sat down at the far end of the table.

It wasn't long before Mrs. Darby came in and welcomed everyone. She sat at the head of the table at the opposite end from us. There was only one empty seat left.

"Mrs. Bennett will be serving supper shortly," Mrs. Darby said in a pleasant voice. "I hope everyone's rooms are satisfactory."

"This place is incredible," Dad said, as his opening to what I knew would become a short speech. Good old Dad. He was never one to hold back. That was probably why he was so successful in business. He always spoke his mind and usually beat everyone else to the punch. "Everything I have seen so far in this quaint town has been more than I could have imagined. As you know, we're from California where the pace is very fast. Here I already get the distinct feeling the pace is much more laid back. I know my family and I will enjoy it here very much. Once we get settled into the Kotter estate, we look forward to hosting backyard barbecues and joining the town festivals."

Just then Dylan came into the dining room and sat in the empty seat next to his mom. "Did you say you're moving into the Kotter estate?" he said with a strange look on his face.

I nearly melted at the sound of his velvety voice. Although we were at opposite ends of the table, he was in clear eye-shot. Great, now I wouldn't be able to take a bite.

"Yes," Dad replied. "There are still a few minor renovations to be completed, but we hope to move in in a couple of days."

"I heard there was construction going on up there," Mrs. Darby said. "I never dreamed it was for your family."

Dad looked puzzled. "Why is it so odd that we're moving into the Kotter estate?"

"Everyone thinks—" Dylan began.

"Everyone thinks it would be nearly impossible to renovate. It was in serious disrepair." Mrs. Darby tossed Dylan a dark stare. "I'm surprised anyone would tackle the repairs necessary to make the estate livable."

"*Au contraire*," Dad said in his fake French accent. "You'd be amazed at what they have accomplished. As a matter of fact, why don't we plan to have you and your son visit as soon as we get settled and you can see the many improvements that have already been made to our new home?"

Well, that was just great. Dad was already trying to play matchmaker.

"That sounds lovely," Mrs. Darby said.

Just then Mrs. Bennett walked through the swinging kitchen door, pushing a cart full of large dinner salads for everyone. Perfect timing. I could sense the conversation taking a turn. I glanced over at Dylan and found him staring at me.

All through dinner I didn't dare look Dylan's way. I was hungry, and I knew if I saw his face I wouldn't be able to eat a thing. The food was amazing, and I gobbled it down right through the scrumptious dessert of fresh apple pie a-la-mode.

"The adults are welcome to join me in the parlor for coffee. It's a good time to get better acquainted," Mrs. Darby, said as she walked toward the parlor room.

Mrs. Bennett followed her with a cart filled with a silver coffee urn and several fancy cups.

Well, I guess that left me out. I stood up and reached for the back of the chair. Dylan, who had somehow made it across the room in a flash, scooted my chair back under the table for me.

"Since the *adults* are going to the parlor for coffee, would you like to take a walk around the grounds with me?" he asked.

"Yes, of course," I replied before my brain had time to weigh the pros and cons of the invitation.

As we walked outside, the sun was just going down behind the large weeping willow tree that stood by a small pond at the front of the property.

"Would you like to sit on the porch swing?" Dylan asked.

I nodded yes.

We crossed the porch to a large white swing with artificial flowers entwined up the chains that held it to the ceiling. I noticed a small sign on the wall next to the entrance: *Darby Lane Bed & Breakfast – Owners Emily & Dillon Darby.*

His name wasn't spelled the same as California Dylan. I let out a quiet sigh of relief.

"Do you have a boyfriend back in California?" Dillon asked.

"My, you do come to the point, don't you?" I was surprised by his directness. "Are all the boys in Indiana like that?"

"Only the ones that want a direct answer," he replied in that dreamy voice. "And I hope that means you'll be honest with me."

"Truth?" I asked.

"Truth."

"Very well." I took a deep breath. "Yes, I had a boyfriend when I left California, but it seems he has moved on."

Dillon's expression seemed more relaxed. "What was his name?"

"You are extremely nosy for having just met me."

"Soooo?" he asked, still waiting for an answer.

"Okay, I'll tell you, but don't laugh," I said. "His name was Dylan."

"You're kidding me, right?" Then he laughed. "Seriously, what was his name?"

"His name was Dylan. D-y-l-a-n."

"Well, at least my name is spelled right," he replied with a grin. "I hope it doesn't remind you of him every time you say my name."

"Hardly," I answered. "You are total opposites."

"Would you care to elaborate on that?" Dillon asked.

"You know, it really doesn't matter. He's there and I'm here and that's that." The conversation was getting a little uncomfortable, so I decided to play his game. "Do you have a girlfriend? What's her name? Does she have long hair or short hair?"

"No, I don't presently have a girlfriend. My last girlfriend's name was Kenzie. She had short hair and brown eyes. I prefer long dark hair and green eyes." He stopped, looking straight at me with that dark gaze. "Do you know anyone who has long dark hair, green eyes, and is in the market for a new boyfriend?"

It took me a moment to regain my composure. "Possibly," I replied, feeling heat on my face.

After that bit of clumsiness, he led me off the porch. We walked around the property for a while, talking about music and movies, and then exchanged phone numbers.

At the edge of the little pond, we sat on the grass.

"What grade will you be in this year?" Dillon asked.

"Junior. What about you?"

"I'll be a senior," he said matter-of-factly. "It's hard to believe school starts in two weeks."

"What?" I sputtered in shock. "School starts in two weeks? It's still only August. There is another month of summer left. Who in their right mind opens school when it's still summer?"

"Yep, in two weeks I'll begin my final year at good old Tri-County High." Dillon folded his fingers behind his head and lay back on the cool grass. All he needed was a fishing pole in one hand and a piece of hay dangling from his mouth to look like a Norman Rockwell painting.

"That's ludicrous to start school in the middle of summer," I quarreled.

"It's not that bad really," he said, sitting up. "There's a big carnival that comes to town the weekend before school starts. All my friends will be there. I'll be glad to introduce you to them. At least this way you'll go into school knowing someone besides me."

"Why if I didn't know better, Mr. Darby, I'd say you just asked me on an unofficial date," I said with a sugar-coated southern accent.

Dillon laughed. "Let's make it official then."

I was almost expecting a small kiss on the cheek, but instead he held out his hand. A handshake? Really? I would go along with the program. Maybe that was how they did things in the Midwest. I placed my hand in his, and we shook on it. Once again his grip lingered. This time I didn't pull away from him.

All of a sudden he jumped up and pulled me up by my hand.

"We'd better get inside before the 'Mom Cop' comes looking for us," Dillon said.

Holding my hand, he walked me to the inn's front door, held the door open for me, and then escorted me to my room.

"Before you go," I said, letting go of his hand, "I have one question."

He gave a shrug. "Okay. Shoot."

"When we were at dinner—I mean supper, you started to say something about the Kotter Estate but your mom interrupted you. What were you going to say?"

"Mom just didn't want me rambling," Dillon said, shifting nervously from one foot to the other.

"Just spit it out. Honesty is a two way street, buddy."

"I was just going to say," he whispered, leaning close, "that everyone thinks the Kotter Estate is haunted. Goodnight and sweet dreams, Molly Greyson."

Wearing an odd smile, Dillon walked down the hallway.

CHAPTER 7

LYING amid piles of ruffles, I stared up at the bed canopy, uncertain how much sleep I would be able to get that night.

I needed to reason my way through the facts at hand and keep a tight grip on reality. I started by analyzing what Dillon had told me.

First, he said everyone *thought* the Kotter Estate was haunted. There was a big difference between thought and knew. If they only thought it was haunted, that meant no one had seen a ghost. Since the estate had been empty a long time, it probably looked like it could be haunted.

Second, what did I really know about Dillon Darby? I had just met him a few hours ago. How could I know if he was telling the truth or just trying to get under my skin? Maybe he liked to pull pranks on innocent young ladies who happened to fall under his muscular spell. Well, I guess I would find out soon enough.

In two days I would be living at Kotter Estate.

* * *

I awoke to sunshine blinding my eyes.

At first the warmth felt like the bright California sun, but when I opened my eyes further I saw the consuming pinkness around me and remembered that I was in Indiana.

Looking down, I realized I had slept in my clothes on top of the fluffy comforter. I had been thinking about what Dillon had said about the estate, when I must have fallen asleep.

It was not going to ruin my day. Mom and I were going shopping in Indianapolis. Thank goodness for at least one big city close enough to offer familiar surroundings. Besides, shopping always cleared my head and helped me refocus.

I headed down for breakfast and found Mom and Dad already at the table. There was only one other couple sitting with them. The other guests from last night must have already left.

"Good morning, sleepyhead," Mom said. "I thought you were going to sleep right through our shopping trip."

"No way," I said, stacking three large pancakes on my plate. After the first heavenly bite, I moaned in approval.

Mrs. Bennett poured me a glass of orange juice, half of which I gulped down in one swallow. Was it me or did the food here just taste better?

"I've decided I'd like a canopy bed for my new room," I said matter-of-factly, finishing off the last bite of pancake.

"You want a canopy bed?' Mom looked stunned. "Does that have anything to do with the one in your room upstairs?"

I shrugged. "New house, new bed."

Mom's mouth dropped open. She had always nagged me to be more feminine, to trade in jeans and baggy sweatshirts for an occasional dress. Now she just might get that wish.

I started to take my plate to the kitchen as usual, when Mrs. Bennett reached for it.

"That's alright, honey, I'll take that for you," Mrs. Bennett said.

I wasn't used to having someone take the dishes for me. Maybe we should look into filling the maid's quarters at our new house.

Mom must have read my mind. "Don't get used to this service, Molly. It's just part of a bed and breakfast. You'll still be putting your dishes in the dishwasher at home."

Just then Dillon came into the dining room. "Enjoy your breakfast?" he asked.

"I have never had pancakes like those before," I replied.

"Good." Dillon looked very pleased. "Glad you enjoyed them. I made them myself."

My mouth dropped open. Handsome and a good cook? Maybe he was the real deal. And maybe he was telling the truth about the house.

* * *

AFTER Mom and I returned from our whirlwind shopping trip in Indianapolis, I dropped the bags filled with jeans and the requisite several pairs of shoes. Then I searched the B&B for Dillon.

He wasn't anywhere to be found. When we were all seated at the table for supper, Mrs. Bennett began serving the first course without Dillon in his usual seat.

Mrs. Darby must have seen me eyeing his seat. "Dillon isn't joining us tonight. His team has basketball practice. They start practices before school starts. People here are very serious about basketball. There was even a movie made about a winning team from Indiana."

Embarrassed that she knew I was looking for her son, I dove into my food and did not look up until I was finished.

After supper, I climbed onto the porch swing. I must have dozed off at some point, because I awoke to loud voices. Startled, I sat up quickly, the swing creaking in the process.

"Guess you have a little California Dreamin' to take care of, huh Darby?" some guy called.

Opening my eyes, I saw Dillon walk away from a car.

"You guys are nuts!" Dillon yelled back over his shoulder. "Go home and stay out of trouble!"

As he walked onto the porch, Dillon saw me sitting on the swing.

"What did they mean by California Dreamin'?" I asked, hoping it was about me.

"Nothing." He looked surprised to see me waiting for him. "They're just needling me, because I decided to come straight home instead of hanging out at the drive-in."

"What time is it?" I asked rubbing my eyes.

"Ten o'clock. That shopping trip must have worn you out," Dillon said with a laugh. "Looks like you fell asleep."

"No, I didn't."

Dillon reached up and touched my cheek. I thought he was being romantic, but instead he pulled off a silk flower that had been stuck to my cheek.

Embarrassed, I straightened my hair back with my hands and felt over the rest of my face for any other foreign objects.

"Come on, sleeping beauty," he said, offering his hand. "I'll walk you inside."

I did not take his outstretched hand. "Wait, I have a couple of questions about what you said last night."

He looked a bit confused. "What did I say?"

"You said the Kotter Estate is haunted."

"Oh. Well, let me clarify that. I said some people 'think' it's haunted. There's been no proof of that. There are some people in this town who claim to be descendants from a long line of past town residents. They grew up here and their father before them and their father before that. They think they know everything about this town, including its history. They have passed down rumors from generation to generation, without questioning them. Some people even think *this* house is haunted."

"This house, too?" I asked, a bit stunned.

"Let me tell you a little story," Dillon said in a serious tone. "A true story."

I settled back in the swing and focused my complete attention on the Adonis in front of me.

"Mom let me invite a few buddies for a sleepover for my thirteenth birthday," he began.

"How old are you now?"

"I'm seventeen." He tossed me a frown. "Do you want to hear this story or not?"

"Sorry, I'll be quiet." I crossed my legs on the swing and faced him. I was more than ready to listen, but had to try very hard not to swoon at the messy hair and rosy cheeks of this gorgeous Indiana farm boy.

"Anyway," Dillon continued, "my old room is actually the room you're staying in. My friends and I were on the floor in sleeping bags, telling all kinds of stupid stories. We heard a noise above us coming from the ceiling. It sounded like footsteps. We all froze. It was dead silence in my room. We didn't hear anything else, so we just passed it off as our imaginations and went on talking. About five minutes later we heard a loud thump. Then more footsteps. The noise had definitely come from the ceiling. None of us wanted to admit we were afraid, so I suggested we go up in the attic together and check it out. There was an attic access door in the back of my closet."

A chill went up my spine at the mention of a door at the back of the closet in the room where I would be sleeping that night.

"Wait," I interrupted. "There's no closet in that room. Only a wardrobe for clothes."

"Precisely." Dillon looked rather perturbed now. "Do you want me to finish or stop here?"

"Sorry," I mumbled and made a locking motion with my fingers at my lips. I tried to shake the vision out of my head of the little door in the closet of my new room at the house.

"The wardrobe covers the closet door," he said. "But I'll get to that later. As I was saying, my closet had a door that led up to the attic. We never went up there, because Mom stored my dad's stuff up there."

"What happened to your—" I stopped midsentence and put both hands over my mouth.

Dillon looked at me with a warning in his eyes and then his expression gentled. "Dad was killed in Afghanistan when I was ten."

After that, I decided to hold all questions until he was finished. If I wanted to get to the end of this story I needed to shut up.

"We walked up the steep staircase together," he said. "It was dark and dusty. I pulled the chain on the old light bulb that hung in the middle of the room. We looked around but didn't find anything odd or ghostly. We all sort of relaxed and started to laugh. We were thirteen. No ghosts were going to get us. As we started toward the stairs I noticed footprints in the dust on the floor. We followed the footprints. They stopped by my dad's army duffle bag. Next to the bag on the floor was his helmet. It looked like it had been dropped as the dust was shifted around it.

"Behind the bag the footprints continued. We followed them until they stopped about two feet from an old standing mirror. Then there was nothing. We looked at each other for a moment. When no one seemed to have an explanation, we headed toward the stairs with me last in line.

"All of a sudden my dad's helmet began rolling toward me. Cold air filled the stairway, as if it were the middle of winter. I freaked and began pushing everyone down the stairs. The helmet followed me, bouncing off each step. As I cleared the door I slammed it shut and heard the helmet slam against the door on the opposite side with a loud crack.

"I ran and got Mom. Each of us tried to tell our version, talking loudly all at once. Mom told everyone to shut up and then asked me to explain. I told her the whole story, from hearing the first footsteps to the helmet chasing us down the stairs. She just blinked, walked over to the door and opened it. There was no helmet. We all looked around in amazement. She asked if we had been telling ghost stories like we always did when we had sleepovers. Then she reassured us it was just our imaginations stirred up by the silly stories.

"We didn't tell anymore stories that night. I turned up the radio to drown out any unwanted noises and we went to sleep. The next day Mom went in the attic. I watched as she removed everything but my Dad's things, including the duffle bag that was tied securely with the helmet inside. That afternoon she hired a construction crew to come in and brick up the opposite side of the door. After locking the attic door, she placed the wardrobe in front of the closet door. Then she moved me into another bedroom.

"That's the day she decided to open our home as a bed and breakfast. She wanted more people around, hoping it would bring new life to the old house. We never spoke of the incident again."

Dillon let out a heavy sigh. He seemed drained of energy.

I sat still, stunned at the story, stunned at the possibility of ghosts.

"Well, nothing to say now, Miss Chatterbox?" Dillon asked.

"I'm blown away that you would share your story with me," I admitted. "So you aren't one of those people who thinks they saw a ghost. You know there are ghosts."

"I never saw a ghost, so I still only think there might be the possibility of such things," Dillon clarified. "And you are the only one besides my buddies and Mom who know about this. I hope you will respect my family and keep this information to yourself. It wouldn't be good for business. And I'm certain your next question will be if I have heard or seen anything since that night. My answer is no. Not a bump or a thump or a single footstep."

Now it seemed all the questions I had before were moot. Dillon seemed stressed and I didn't want to prolong the agony by asking more stupid questions or dredging up old memories of his dad. And I certainly didn't want to share with him that the closet in my new room also had a small door in the very back.

Dillon walked me to my room, but before he left he touched my cheek with his palm. It was rough like that of a man who worked hard using his hands. It was nothing like the hands of the boys from California. The hardest jobs their hands did were holding the steering wheels of their sleek little convertibles or gripping their perfectly waxed surfboards.

I knew Dad had gotten the green light from John and that we were moving into the estate tomorrow. It would be a busy day.

One thing I planned to do was find a way to unlock that strange little door at the back of my closet. Was it also an attic access? If not, where did it lead?

But first I had to get through one more night in Dillon's old room, the one he thought was haunted.

CHAPTER 8

MY eyes wouldn't stay shut.

I had slept in this room the night before without any problems. Now after hearing Dillon's ghost story, all I could do was stare at the ceiling of ruffles above me and listen for every sound.

I couldn't stand it. I got out of bed and walked toward the menacing wardrobe. I opened the double doors and inspected the interior. It was empty except for a few wire hangers. I had not put any of my clothes inside it. I laid my shoulder along the side, planted my feet squarely, and pushed with all my strength. It wouldn't budge.

Of course, it wouldn't move. Why would it? My one hundred and one pounds couldn't possibly move a three hundred pound solid oak wardrobe. Besides, if a ghost wanted out of the attic a brick wall or wooden wardrobe wasn't going to stop it.

I returned to the soft bed, allowing my head to sink deep into the feather pillows. Then I stared up again and waited for anything to convince me this place was haunted.

Before I knew it, I heard birds chirping outside the window. I leaned over to check the time on my phone. Seven o'clock. Yikes! I must have fallen asleep after all.

I got dressed in a hurry and crammed my few things into my backpack. I stopped by the unoccupied community bathroom and splashed water on my face. I threw on a little mascara and added a couple swipes of blush across my cheeks. I pulled my hair up in a ponytail, while my toothbrush hung from my mouth. I knew Dad wanted to check out by eight o'clock, but I had forgotten to set my alarm. In order to get one more helping of Dillon's pancakes, I had to multi-task.

As I headed for the stairs I realized I had left my phone in the bedroom on the night stand. I quickly returned to the bedroom and found my phone.

Turning to leave, I heard a loud thump.

I froze and scanned the room.

Silence.

I took a step. Still nothing.

It must have been people downstairs preparing to leave. Feeling silly, I headed toward the door.

A creaking sound echoed and again I froze. Turning, I saw one of the wardrobe doors ease open a few inches. From where I stood, I could faintly make out an object on the floor of the wardrobe, which last night I was sure had been empty. Just as I was about to push open the small door for a closer look, my phone vibrated sending small waves of tremors through my hand.

Startled, I nearly dropped my phone. I looked down and saw it was Dad texting me.

Bolting out of the room, I slammed the door behind me and made it downstairs in a flash. In a rush, I pushed open the double glass doors of the dining room and startled everyone at the table. All eyes were on me, including Dillon's.

"Sorry," I said to Dillon, avoiding the room full of disapproving eyes. "I overslept and was afraid I would miss these scrumptious pancakes."

I slipped into my seat next to Mom and looked down at my hands. I could feel that my face was flushed. I glanced over at Dillon, who was still looking at me. I could tell by his expression that he knew something was wrong.

"Well, that's the fastest you've ever responded to one of my texts," Dad said in a jovial tone, but he was eying me with suspicion.

"Grab a stack of those 'scrumptious pancakes' and let's eat outside on the porch," Dillon said.

I definitely wanted to get away from all those scrutinizing eyes. I forked three exceptionally large pancakes, grabbed the personal syrup container, and followed Dillon. He was balancing his plate and two large glasses of orange juice, as he stood by the door.

"Eat fast!" Dad shouted as the screen door swung shut behind me. "I want to check out by eight o'clock."

When we had settled ourselves at the small table on the porch, Dillon tossed me a curious look. I poured the syrup over my already butter drenched pancakes and stuffed the first delicious bite into my mouth.

Dillon just stared at me.

"What?" I asked between bites.

"What do you mean, 'what'?" His tone was rather sharp. "You burst into the dining room like you had seen a ghost."

I swallowed a large gulp of orange juice. "No, I didn't see a ghost. We don't believe in ghosts, right?"

"You're not getting off that easy, Molly Greyson," Dillon grumbled.

"I may have only met you two days ago, but I can read your face like a book. There's definitely something wrong."

"I heard a thump in your old room this morning," I replied with as much nonchalance as I could manage. "I think there was something sitting on the floor of the wardrobe that wasn't there yesterday."

Dillon's mouth dropped open.

"Doesn't matter," I continued. "I'm leaving in a little while, and it's not my problem."

"What do you mean it doesn't matter?" Dillon echoed. "What did you see in the wardrobe?"

I did not appreciate his tone of voice. "Fine, I'll tell you. I think it was a helmet."

"That's impossible," Dillon said in a forceful voice.

He jerked me up by my arm, and we headed around the side of the house to the back.

"Where are we going?" I asked, as I poked one more bite into my mouth.

"We're going up to my old room to check this out," he said with determination.

I dug my heels into the porch deck and bucked like a mule. "I'm not going back into that room. I know I saw something in that wardrobe that wasn't there before. And thanks to your story it totally freaked me out."

"We'll take the back stairs, so no one will know," Dillon said, dragging me along.

"Wait," I snapped, jerking my arm out of iron his grip. "I said I'm not going back up to that room."

"We need to prove that there isn't a helmet," Dillon said. "And that there are no ghosts."

He grabbed my arm again, and we made our way toward the back stairs.

"Fine," I muttered, following behind him.

When we got to the room, the door was ajar.

"I know I slammed that door behind me," I whispered.

There was movement in the room. Dillon pushed at the door to open it for a better look.

"Morning to you, Mr. Darby," the lady said. "Just straightening up a bit before our next guests arrive."

"Morning, Mrs. Rose," Dillon replied in a casual tone. "Molly thinks she left something in the wardrobe. We're just coming to check."

He walked over to the wardrobe, practically dragging me behind him.

He opened both doors. It was empty except for a few wire hangers. He turned and gave me puzzled look.

All I could do was stare into the empty cabinet.

"Thanks, Mrs. Rose," he said. "Guess it's not here. We'll get out of your way now."

Dillon excused us and we left the room.

"Okay, Molly, you've got some explaining to do," Dillon said in anger. "That's a pretty cruel trick to play on me."

"What are you talking about?"

"Just because I told you my story about the night we heard footsteps and saw the helmet it doesn't give you the right to play games with my memories." There was true pain in his voice.

"I'm not making this up," I vowed. "I heard a thump and I saw what I'm pretty sure was a helmet inside the wardrobe. I'm not trying to hurt you. But if that's what you think of me, then—then it's time for me to leave. Besides, how do I know it's not you playing a trick on me, Mr. Wise Guy?"

I turned and stormed down the back stairs. I passed my half-full plate of cold pancakes sitting on the porch table and went into the lobby. Mom and dad were just checking out.

"There you are," Mom said. "We were just about to go look for you."

I grabbed my backpack, slung it over my shoulder, and headed toward the tank.

"Good riddance," I shouted back over my shoulder.

I had to get into the SUV before the tears started to fall.

CHAPTER 9

IT was only eight miles to the estate, but it seemed like eight hundred.

Corn fields went on and on in endless rows of green arms reaching toward the sky. I saw the silky strands on the top of the stalks and knew they were about ready for de-tasseling. How did a California-born girl know that informational morsel on the life of an ear of corn? Dillon. How did I know it was exactly eight miles from the Bed and Breakfast to my house? Dillon.

As much as I tried, I couldn't get him out of my head. I should be mad at him. He didn't believe me when I told him about seeing what looked like a helmet in the wardrobe. Could I have been wrong? I had not opened the curtains in the room, so the lighting hadn't been great. I was at least fifteen feet away, so the angle wasn't that good, either. Had his story stirred up wild images in my head? Had my imagination simply run away with me?

No, at every turn I had experienced something unexplainable since running into that stupid Gypsy.

I punched Dillon's name on my phone and it began to ring. It went straight to voice mail.

"I think I owe you an apology," I said into the phone. "Please call."

As I pulled the phone from my ear, I looked out the window. The gargoyles on the iron gates seemed more menacing today. Had it been this foreboding the last time? Or was the gloom of the impending storm rising in the morning sky giving it a creepy glow? Dillon had described how the sky looked when there was a possibility of tornados. Several had ravaged the local area a few years ago and had taken out some of the town buildings. I had never seen a tornado and was pretty certain I didn't want to. These clouds were not the black depths that held all the right elements to concoct a swirling devil. They held rain, the heavy downpour kind. Nevertheless, the sky accentuated the eeriness of my new home.

An eighteen-wheeler moving van sat across the span of the circular drive, blocking the main entrance. The driver looked frustrated, as we pulled up next to him.

Dad waved a friendly hello and wheeled the SUV through the bridge-like structure that connected the house with a four car detached garage. Why we needed a four car garage was beyond me, but it came with the estate. It looked newer due to recent renovations. Dad explained that it had originally been a carriage house, built before people had cars. Back then they used carriages pulled by horses for transportation. That explained the broken down barn behind the house.

"Everybody out!" Dad shouted. "We're home."

Easy for him to say. He was pumped up about a new job, new employees, and this massive house. Mom smiled, but I could tell she was a bit apprehensive. She had been a successful interior designer in California, but the market for interior designers in this town seemed slim to non-existent. Dad had told Mom she could redecorate the house to her liking. He had reassured her that Indianapolis was only a short distance away and would provide plenty of new clientele eager for her unique style and design. I saw her face when we had walked in the house the first time. She definitely had her work cut out for her.

I had a new room, a new school, and hopefully would find some new friends. I wasn't exactly the most out-going person, but meeting Dillon had been easy. That was due mostly to his laid-back personality, which likely was a result of being raised in a small town environment. He didn't seem to be in too much of a hurry about anything. My natural instincts were move-it, move-it. Go here. Get there. Don't be late. I had told Dillon I needed to learn to chill like him. He had responded with an honest: "I'm not really chilly, but if you need a fan I can get you one." What pure innocence!

I slipped out of the back seat and tossed my backpack across my shoulder. The sky decided to open up at that very moment and let loose with pouring rain. A flash of lightning tore across the sky. A couple of seconds later a crack of thunder rattled the countryside.

I followed my parents through a covered walkway. Cold sheets of rain buffeted us, while Dad unlocked the back entrance of the house. With the wind howling, we hurried inside out of the rain and let the door slam shut behind us.

What room was this? It was small with a row of hooks set about eyelevel and then shelves below that.

"This is just wonderful," Dad commented happily, shaking the rain from his jacket. "We have our very own mud room."

Whoopee! A mud room. Whatever that was.

I walked through the overrated little mud room and entered a huge kitchen. Some of our boxes were already stacked in the corner. This was one room that made my Mom's eyes shine. She loved to bake, and this was the ultimate kitchen for her. I was glad she had found something attractive about the new house.

The doorbell rang. I let Dad answer it, figuring it was the movers.

It took him a few minutes to get from the kitchen to the front of the house given the mass of the building.

"Molly, it's for you!" Dad called, drawing out the 'you' in a sing-song manner.

I couldn't imagine who would be asking for me. I found my way to the front room and skidded to a stop when I looked out the open door.

It was Dillon. He stood on the large front porch, dripping wet from the storm.

"Dillon, I wasn't expecting you." Grabbing his sleeve, I pulled him inside the house. "Get in here and dry off."

Mom walked up beside me and handed Dillon a towel. "One of the bathroom boxes ended up in the kitchen," she said with a shrug.

"Thought I'd come help you get settled into your new room," Dillon said. He wiped his face with the towel, pushing long dark hair out of those deep green eyes.

"I just, well, I thought you were—"

"Mad at you?" he finished my sentence. "Nope. I'm not mad. Even if I were, I don't stay mad long. Life's too short."

How old was this guy, seventeen or seventy?

The movers pushed past Dillon with a four-wheel cart loaded with boxes. The rain had stopped almost as quickly as it had begun, and the sun peeked out from behind ominous clouds.

"That's odd," I said. "It pours for five minutes. Then the sun comes out."

"Not odd for Indiana," Dillon commented. "The rain can turn on and off like a faucet. You might even see all four seasons in one day."

"Did you get my voice message?" I asked.

"Yes," he replied, "and I accept your apology. Now where's this round room you seem to be so proud of?"

He headed toward the stairs. I practically had to run to keep up with him. His long legs took two steps at a time. When he reached the landing where the stairs split going in opposite directions, he stopped and I nearly ran into him. He turned and surveyed the lower hall.

"Oooowee," he intoned. "This place is amazing."

"You've never been here before?"

"Nope, never," he replied. "I assume your room is this way, since the tower is on this side of the house."

He climbed the rest of the stairs in a normal manner, not two steps at a time. He must have noticed I had difficulty keeping up with him on the first round of stairs.

"The realtor said this place is like a museum to this town, a landmark," I said, climbing the stairs next to him. "I assumed everyone had been here one time or another. I heard some of the past owners held lavish parties in the ballroom on the third floor."

"There's a ballroom?" Dillon looked impressed.

I couldn't understand why Dillon didn't know much about the house. It was supposedly built by the founder of the town.

"Doesn't the town hold celebrations?" I asked.

"Actually, we celebrate something every summer. And no to your next question. There has never been a big town party up here. The place has been vacant as long as I can remember. Come to think of it, I don't recall this house ever being occupied."

That meant no one had lived here for almost two decades. Why would such a magnificent house be left empty for so long? Wait. Hadn't the realtor said it had only been vacant a couple of years?

When we reached the second floor Dillon stopped.

"Which door is yours?" he asked.

"None of these. My room is on the third floor," I said, skipping toward the hidden stairway. "Be careful. The carpet on these stairs is old and loose. They still have a few things to fix, but Mom wants to keep some original stuff. I'm afraid that might include this faded old carpet."

Once we reached the third floor, it was obvious which door was mine. It was the only one up there, and it was rounded to match the shape of the room.

"I'm just guessing, but could *that* door be yours?" Dillon asked, pointing to the rounded door.

I smacked him on the shoulder. "Yes, smarty pants. How very clever you are!"

Dillon entered the room first and looked around. Then he walked over to the round windows and peered out over the grounds. "Awesome view." He turned and nodded toward the back of the room. "What's behind that door?"

"The bathroom," I replied. "Originally, there were eight bedrooms, but no bathrooms. Recent owners changed that to five bedrooms with three bathrooms." At least I knew some history of the house.

Dillon walked over to the door and pushed it open. His mouth dropped, when he took in the size of the room. "Nice."

Then Dillon looked at the other door in the room. He didn't ask what was behind that door. He already knew. We stood close together, arms brushing easily. Neither of us moved or said a word for at least three whole minutes.

"Okay," Dillon said, breaking the silence, "this must be a closet."

"Yes," I said slowly. "It's my closet."

"Is there—"

I nodded in response. I knew the rest of the question.

We stood there in silence for a couple of more minutes.

"This is ridiculous," I said, frustrated with Dillon for making me feel freaked out.

Walking over to the closet, I opened its door. I pulled the chain, and light filled the chamber. The old rolled up musty carpet was gone, and the wood floors were polished. The small door at the back of the closet seemed to stare at us.

I could tell Dillon wasn't too keen on entering the closet, but he put back his shoulders and walked right up to the small door in the back. He jiggled the handle. Locked, just like before.

"Guess no one wants you in here," he said with a shrug.

"Well, I intend to get inside. I want to know what's behind there. Wouldn't you if you were me?"

"It's probably an attic access door like the one I had in my closet," he said. "Sometimes it's best to leave locked doors locked."

Dillon walked out of the closet, pulling the chain as he left.

I stood in the dark closet, baffled by his reaction.

Was his nonchalance an act to cover up fear or was he truly not interested? Did he really believe in ghosts and just didn't want to admit it? Did I believe in ghosts?

Mom stepped into the bedroom and pointed the movers toward the windows. "Your fancy bed has arrived, Molly. I assume you want it centered in the room by the windows."

"Yes, that's perfect," I said.

"Dillon, your mom just called and asked if you were here," Mom informed. "She tried to call your cell phone, but it went to voice mail. She needs you to come home. There's a crowd of people checking in and she needs your help."

Then Mom flitted out the door in a hurry to keep up with the movers.

"Sorry, Molly, I had every intention of helping you settle in today,"

Dillon said as he checked his phone. "Man, I set it to vibrate and forgot to turn it back on. Would it be alright if I came back tomorrow to help?"

"Of course," I said in a flirty voice. "Your mom needs your help. The movers will set up all the big stuff. I'll save the wonderful experience of unpacking for next time."

"Perfect," Dillon said. "Count me in."

As he walked out the door, he turned and gave a very adorable wink. Then he was gone.

I sat down hard on one of the boxes and tried not to swoon. Really, I did try.

As expected, the movers had my bed set up in no time. Mom and I had picked out a ruffled comforter with sheets that were a close match to the one at the B&B. Mom was so happy that my room was going to be an ocean of pink, the perfect daughter colors. In all honesty, I had grown tired of the harsh black and teal that was my old bedroom in California. I loved the warmth of the oak wood floors and soft pink walls here. I had done a one eighty and was accepting the move a lot better than expected. Of course, Dillon had a lot to do with that.

Who would have thought a week ago that this California girl would be happy in the middle of a cornfield?

* * *

DAD brought home carryout from a diner in town.

It was like a homemade dinner complete with cornbread. Mom hadn't had time to shop for food, but that was on her agenda for tomorrow. My agenda was to have Dillon help me unpack.

Tired and full from dinner, or supper, I decided to give my antique bath tub a try. Mom and I had picked up scented bubble bath during our shopping spree. I poured some into the hot steaming water. Bubbles began to grow in a dancing rainbow of colors. The warmth of the water combined with the bubbles made me feel like a princess. I played with the bubbles, using my toes. I was beginning to like this new me.

I heard a faint voice.

"Is that you Mom?" I shouted through the closed bathroom door.

Again I heard a voice. It sounded like someone calling my name, but I couldn't make out the words. The voice was definitely female.

I pulled a towel from the rack and wrapped it around me.

Peeking out the door, I realized it wasn't Mom. The stereo was on. I could have sworn I had turned it off before getting into the tub.

Too tired to worry about it, I slipped on pajamas and left the steamy bathroom.

The bedroom felt chilly, almost cold. I jumped into my new bed and pulled the covers up around my neck. Snuggling into the soft warmth of my new canopy bed, I stared up at pink ruffles.

There was a soft knock on my door. Then Mom came in and kissed me on the forehead, like she had done when I was little. "Are you going to be okay way up here in this gigantic bed?"

"I'm fine," I answered with a big yawn. "Just really tired."

"Goodnight," Mom said and then left the bedroom.

I rolled over and let my head sink into the softness of the pillow.

As I was drifting off to sleep, I thought I heard a door creaking. Drowsiness convinced me I was already asleep and dreaming.

Dreaming of doors with strange little locks.

CHAPTER 10

CONSIDERING all the crazy stuff tumbling around in my brain, I had slept well.

I stretched and yawned. It was the first day in our new house and Dillon was coming over to help me unpack. Just the thought of him gave me goose-bumps.

I reached for my phone to check the time. It was already eight thirty. Dillon was an early riser. It seemed everyone here got up at the crack of dawn.

Wait. Did I smell pancakes? Was Dillon already here?

Hopeful, I raced into the bathroom, brushed my teeth, and pulled my ponytail into a messy bun. I skidded out of the bathroom, my socks slipping easily across the wood floor. Then I stumbled to a halt.

The closet door stood open a few inches. I tiptoed over to it. As I pushed it shut, a familiar creaking echoed. I was certain I had heard that same sound last night.

Nonsense. The house had my imagination running wild.

The smell of warm syrup filled my nostrils, redirecting my attention to my rumbling stomach. Without another thought, I headed down the steep stairs in search of breakfast.

As I pushed open the swinging door to the kitchen, I saw Dillon standing at the stove. He had a spatula in his hand. A stack of pancakes sat on the counter next to him. Mom sat at the breakfast bar with a hot cup of coffee and a plate of pancakes in front of her.

"Good morning, Miss Greyson," Dillon said in a butler-type voice. "Your breakfast waits."

"Dillon showed up a little while ago with all the ingredients to fix us this wonderful meal," Mom said, sipping her steaming coffee. "He must have snooped in our refrigerator yesterday to see we hadn't been to the store yet. Wasn't this the most perfect neighborly thing to do?"

Well, considering Dillon lived eight miles away, I'd say neighborly was stretching it a bit. But I was very grateful for the yummy pancakes. Somehow the carryout leftovers didn't sound very appealing.

"Thanks," I said, as Dillon sat a stack of pancakes in front of me and a cup of warm syrup. I dug in and then realized he was watching me. "What, you're not joining us?"

Dillon reached for his coffee and sat down next to me at the bar. "I ate hours ago. Had a few chores to do for Mom before I came over. I did promise I'd help you unpack today. We're still on, aren't we?"

"Oh yes," Mom chimed in, interrupting. "Before I forget, John left keys for all of us. He said for some reason every inside door has a lock on it but each one is the same. He called it a skeleton key." Mom handed me a large oddly shaped key. "Here's your key in case you get locked out of that enormous bathroom of yours, heaven forbid."

I turned and looked at Dillon. His expression was priceless.

I dangled the key at Dillon, taunting him. "Well, there's no time like the present to open that little baby up and see what's on the other side."

After finishing my pancakes in record time, I grabbed a cup of coffee and then headed upstairs with Dillon at my heels.

"If we're going to do this, at least give me the key," Dillon said, plucking the key from my hand. "I wouldn't want you running into anything unexpected."

When we walked into the room, I was mortified that I had left the place in such a mess. I had not planned on Dillon arriving so early. I quickly straightened and shoved things around until I felt it was a little more presentable.

"Don't do that on my account," he said. "You should see my room in the morning. Not a pretty sight."

I opened the closet door and shoved aside some of the boxes I had already placed in there. The hidden door seemed larger somehow.

Dillon aimed the key toward the hole beneath the knob, but his hand shook and the key dropped onto the floor with a muffled *clink*.

"Do I need to do this?" I asked.

"No," he said, defensively. "I've got this. The key is just a little slippery."

With a slow twist, the sound of tumblers moving assured us that it had worked. Dillon pulled the key from the hole and looked up at me. I was hovering over him like a mother hen.

"Who wants to do the honors?" he asked.

I hesitated a second. "Since it's my room, I should open it."

My fingers gripped the brass knob. It was cold and unwelcoming to the touch. I turned it and heard a soft click. I pulled the knob, and the door creaked open with a low groan.

We both took a step back and stared at a crudely constructed brick wall. In many places the cement had crumbled between the bricks, leaving gaps that allowed a musty order to escape. We both waved our hands in front of our noses to push away the stale smell.

"Coincidence?" I asked, but I really didn't believe that.

From the look on Dillon's face, it seemed he that didn't, either.

"I don't know," he said with a shrug. "Mom bricked off my door only four years ago. This looks like it's been bricked up for decades."

He poked at the mortar. Pieces fell to the floor, making one of the gaps even wider. A puff of dust escaped through the opening making us both sneeze.

Suddenly, cold air surrounded us.

Grabbing an old sock out of one of the boxes, I stuffed it in the hole.

"Okay, I've seen enough for today." I shut the door and turned the key, relocking it. Once again the tumblers made their clinking sound. Just to make sure, I tried the knob. It was locked. "We need to talk about what we're going to do next."

"What we're going to do next? What does that mean?" Dillon looked perplexed. "I'd say the decision has been made for us. It's locked and bricked shut. We aren't meant to be on the other side of that door."

"But—"

"No buts. Leave it alone, Molly." Dillon shoved me out of the closet. "It's for the best. Don't go searching for trouble."

He looked around my room for a moment, as if searching for something. Then he grabbed my large framed mirror and dragged it into the closet. He pushed it to the very back and centered it in front of the door.

"Now, you don't have to look at it every time you come in here," he said.

"I might not see it," I argued, "but I'll still know it's there."

"For now. Eventually you'll forget about it. I did." Dillon then looked at stacks of boxes marked *Molly's Room*. "So where do we begin?"

I folded my arms and stiffened into a defensive stance. "Okay, Mr. Darby, I'll let it go for now. But this is not over. Not by a long shot."

"I know, I know. But let's just enjoy the day and not let any ghost stories spoil it."

* * *

WE spent the rest of the morning unpacking boxes and putting away stuff.

We talked about everything from school to movies. He told me about his friends and reminded me of the carnival that was coming to town this weekend. Everyone from Tri-County High School would be there. He said it would be a great chance for me to meet the gang. In California 'gang' had a much different meaning than in Indiana, but I didn't tell Dillon that.

"Earth to Molly," Dillon said. "Are you ready to meet my friends on Saturday?"

"What? Oh, yes. Of course. It should be fun." My mind had wondered off.

It wasn't as easy as Dillon said it would be to forget about the bricked up door. I wish I had never opened it. Then I wouldn't have seen the bricks and wouldn't be racking my brain trying to explain it.

I laid a stack of t-shirts on my dresser, knocking my purse onto the floor in the process. A few things scattered out of the open end. Dillon, gentleman that he was, reached down and gathered up the mess. He returned everything except a card.

He stood for a moment, looking at the card. "Your journey will end where the once living still tread," he read aloud. "Steer clear of the visions in the darkness for they are the ghosts of lost souls. Beware Molly Greyson, beware of." With a scowl he looked up at me and waved the card. "What is this?"

I snatched the card from his hand and shoved it into my jeans pocket. "It's nothing. Just some stupid card I got when I was in Las Vegas."

"If it's nothing and it's stupid, then why are you keeping it?"

"Fine," I snapped. I pulled the card from my pocket and threw it in the box we had designated as trash. "Happy?"

Dillon looked a bit unsure. "Are you certain you don't believe in ghosts?"

"Of course not. Why would a silly card cause me to believe in ghosts?" I needed to direct his attentions somewhere other than talk of ghosts. "Let's get something to eat. I'm starved."

"Sounds good to me," he said, reaching for the box. "I'll carry the trash down, so you won't have to do it later."

"No!" I hadn't meant to shout at him, but for some reason I couldn't lose that card. "I'll get it later."

Dillon dropped the box onto the floor. "Okay, but remember me when you're struggling to haul it downstairs."

* * *

MOM had been to the grocery, while we had been knee deep in jeans and t-shirts upstairs. She had sandwiches ready for us when we entered the kitchen.

I pulled the refrigerator open to find it fully stocked. Finally! While we ate, Mom asked how my room organization was going. Dillon chimed in that he had offered to carry my trash down, but I had refused.

"I forgot to tell you there's a dumbwaiter in your bathroom," Mom said. "As a matter of fact, there are dumbwaiters in all of the bathrooms. I assume they are for laundry, because they seem to empty out into the basement where the maid's old laundry room was. I'm glad the last residents moved the laundry room up to the main level. I checked out the basement earlier. It's pretty disgusting. The less I have to go down there, the better."

This house had a basement? Doom filled my head. Basements were not among my favorite things.

"Why didn't I see the door in my bathroom?" I asked.

"The one in our bathroom is hidden in the wallpaper design," Mom explained. "I'm certain yours must be the same."

Dillon and I looked at each other. It was like a light bulb went off for both of us. Together, we jumped up and raced up the stairs to my third level bathroom. We searched the wallpaper feeling every bump, as we slid our hands over the antique design.

"Found it!" Dillon announced with excitement.

The dumbwaiter door was camouflaged among the large wallpaper flowers and hidden behind a wicker towel stand.

Dillon pushed aside the towel stand, exposing a little door. Instead of a knob, it had a small latch. Beneath the latch was a key hole matching the rest of the doors.

I ran and got the skeleton key.

Without hesitating, I shoved the key in the hole and turned it. A grinding sound like rusty metal screeched, making me grit my teeth. Then the familiar sound of clinking tumblers echoed. I pulled open the door.

There were no bricks this time. A large cloud of dust rose from the darkness, causing me to cough.

Together, we stuck our heads inside the door. Enough light from the bathroom shone inside to reveal a small elevator with a wooden floor and manual pulleys. There was nothing electrical or twenty-first century about this antique contraption.

That same peculiar musty order we had noticed in the closet now oozed out at us. Repulsed by the smell, I shut the door.

I looked at Dillon. We both knew what we had to do. We had to load something onto the dumbwaiter and work the pulleys to send it downward. Then we had to go into the basement and check it out.

I hated basements.

Dillon looked around the bathroom and then picked up my hair dryer.

I shook my head no. Absolutely not. I grabbed two rolls of toilet paper and placed them on the platform of the ancient dumbwaiter.

"Really?" Dillon said with a smile.

"I can replace toilet paper," I said, defending my choice. "I need my hair dryer."

"Will the rolls be heavy enough?" Dillon asked.

"We'll soon find out," I replied.

I tugged at the pulleys. At first the old elevator moved in awkward jerks, but as I continued to pull the ropes the motion became more fluid. We stuck our heads in the little elevator closet and watched as the toilet paper disappeared down into the darkness. It wasn't long before the ropes began to show slack.

"We must have hit bottom," Dillon said. "Let's go check it out."

We turned and headed out the door. Then I stopped suddenly.

"I have no idea how to get to the basement," I admitted.

"Your mom does," Dillon said, as we turned toward the stairs.

We found Mom still in the kitchen, putting the rest of the groceries in the pantry.

"Where's the door to the basement?" I asked.

Mom looked puzzled. "Really, Molly? You actually want to go down there? You hate basements."

I gave her my best evil eye, and she quickly pointed us in the direction of the basement.

The basement door was located in the mud room just outside the kitchen. Dillon pulled on the knob. Like everything else in this house, it was locked.

"What's up with the doors in this place?" Dillon grumbled. "It's like someone doesn't want us snooping around."

I handed Dillon the key, and he did the honors.

My palms began to sweat, as my mind wandered back to an event twelve years earlier. If my cousin, Patrick, hadn't have locked me in Great-grandma's basement when I was four, maybe I wouldn't be so afraid now. Her basement hadn't been old and creepy, but it had been a life changing experience to a four-year-old alone in a big dark room with only small windows out of reach. I had screamed so loud for so long that my voice was practically gone by the time she had found me. All I could do was point at Patrick and cry.

"Molly, are you going with me or not?"

The sound of Dillon's voice broke the spell that had me frozen on the landing.

I shook the bad memories out of my head. Before us was a small dark room with what looked like yet another door about six feet ahead. Dillon searched for a light switch. He found an odd looking box with two buttons on it. He pushed a button and a very dull light came on overhead. I switched on the flashlight that I had picked up for this adventure.

Dillon didn't even check the door knob. He just inserted the key into the lock and turned it. *Click.* Obviously it had been locked as well.

He pushed open the door and a familiar dank smell made my nose burn. I covered my nose with my hand and peered into the murkiness. Dillon flipped a nearby light switch. A bulb flickered to life, illuminating a set of wooden stairs with a room at the bottom.

"Good," he said. "At least we can see where we're going." He started down the wooden steps and then turned. "Coming?"

I gripped the flashlight and followed Dillon down the steps.

"Be careful," he warned. "Looks like a few of the steps are rotted through."

I avoided the holes in the steps and soon found myself in the middle of a dirt floor basement. There seemed to be several rooms to the right, but in this light it was hard to tell. One thing was for certain. I had no intention of checking them out.

As we walked through the dimly lit openness, we saw what looked like an old tub near the corner of the room. Next to the tub was the small elevator with my two rolls of toilet paper.

Dillon laughed out loud. "So the dumbwaiter does work. This must be where the maids used to do laundry. Let's look around."

"Really, Dillon, we know where the dumbwaiter goes already." I pulled at the back of his shirt. "Let's go back upstairs. This smell is making me sick."

Ignoring me, he headed to the back of the room where the lighting wasn't as good. I really didn't want to go any deeper into this hole, but I also didn't want to stand here alone. I hurried and caught up with him just as he stopped.

"Give me the flashlight," he said.

I handed him the flashlight, and he shined it ahead of him.

There was a large hole about halfway up a brick wall. Crumbling bricks and wads of mortar were scattered on the floor. It looked like someone had broken the wall on purpose.

Dillon moved closer to the hole. I followed right on his heels.

He shined the flashlight into the hole. "What are those things?"

Mumbling to himself, he stepped closer to the hole. Then without warning, he backed up stepping on my toes.

"Ouch," I grumbled. "What's wrong? What did you see?"

"A rat. I hate rats." Dillon gave an exaggerated shudder.

"Now we're even," I said, heading back toward the stairs. "I hate basements. You hate rats. No need to come back here. Ever. Agreed?"

"Agreed," he said, scratching his head. "But don't you think it odd that the bricks are on the floor outside the hole? I mean, if someone tried to knock a hole in the wall from here, the bricks would fall inside the hole. These bricks are all over the floor here, like the hole was made from the other side."

"I'm not going to stand here and analyze a hole in the wall," I said. "I just want to get out of here. But I do need to tell Dad to get an exterminator. I wonder what attracted rats. Did you see anything in that opening?"

"Just some blocks of cement with letters on them. Nothing that should attract a rat. Unless…."

"Unless what?"

"Unless the blocks of cement were gravestones," he said in a quiet voice.

"That's ridiculous," I said. "You're just trying to make me freak out again. You are not in the least bit funny."

I stomped up the stairs with Dillon following close behind.

"Sorry," I apologized, once I reached the top. "I didn't mean to jump down your throat. Basements give me the creeps. Let's just forget it."

"Forgotten," he said, but he still looked a little upset. "By the way, we need to talk about the carnival next week."

Scenarios of how he was going to get out of taking me to the carnival filled my brain.

As I locked the basement door, I had to choke back tears. "It's okay if you don't want to go. I understand."

"There you go, jumping to conclusions, Miss Greyson. Just be quiet and listen."

I swallowed my pride and stood, quietly listening.

"I was going to say I am going to a basketball camp at a University in Ohio next week, but I'll be home on Saturday in time for the carnival. It's my opportunity to be seen by NBA coaches and maybe earn a college scholarship." He stopped and grabbed my hand. "But I'll be back to take you to the carnival. I'm not about to miss our first official date."

Boy, did I feel like a jerk. All I could do was nod, as a single tear rolled down my cheek. He wiped away the tear with his finger.

I cleared my throat and blinked back any more tears that might threaten to fall. "Well, the basement mystery is solved. But I forgot to bring the toilet paper back with me."

"Good thing I didn't put the hair dryer on the elevator," Dillon said with a grin.

Dillon's handsome face with that crooked little grin made the basement and the dumbwaiter seem less threatening.

If only it could do the same for strange brick walls.

CHAPTER 11

THE rest of the day went all too quickly.

My room looked as if I had lived there for years. The pink was a little overwhelming, but it made me feel feminine. Or maybe that was Dillon's effect on me. Whatever it was, I liked it. It was a far cry from the skateboarding ball cap girl from California.

My phone rang. When I saw the caller ID, I nearly fainted. It was Dylan from California.

"Are you going to answer it or stare at it?" Dillon asked.

"No, I don't think—"

"Answer the phone," Dillon grumbled. "From the look on your face, you already know who it is."

Reluctantly, I pushed the accept button.

"Hello?" I squeaked out.

A peculiar expression crossed Dillon's face.

I couldn't imagine why the other Dylan would be calling me, but as he rambled on and on in my ear I only heard about every other word. My mind was fixed on the Dillon standing before me, listening to one end of the conversation. All I could squeeze out were some uh-huhs and wows.

After a moment, Dillon made a waving signal with his hand.

"No, don't go, Dillon!" I shouted.

"I'm not going anywhere, Molly," came through phone.

"Not you, Dylan," I snapped with the phone pressed to my ear.

Indiana Dillon must have realized that the person on the other end of the phone was California Dylan. He pointed down as if to say he would go downstairs and let me have my privacy.

Don't leave, I mouthed.

He nodded and shut the door behind him.

Dylan had continued talking through it all, without missing a beat. "So, Molly, you haven't answered my question."

"I'm sorry," I said, but I really wasn't. "I'm surprised you called. The last time we talked I thought we had said our good-byes."

"I asked if I could come visit you in Indiana," he said. "You didn't give me an answer."

It was that old Dylan sweet and innocent voice I had heard so many times before. It dawned on me that was the voice he had always used to get me to do what he wanted.

"That's not a good idea," I said, trying to shake that sticky sweet voice out of my head. "School starts here in two weeks. I need to focus."

"School starts out there in two weeks? Bummer. I could fly out sooner. Dad said he'd let me use the company jet." Dylan was practically begging now, which was out of character for him.

Plastic people with their money. Then I realized that only two weeks ago I had been one of those people.

I didn't feel like a girl from California anymore. That girl was already gone, lost in a sea of pink. Then I put two and two together and realized why Dylan was calling. His new girlfriend didn't work out and he wanted me back because it would be too much work to break in a new girlfriend. I was familiar, even if I was two thousand miles away. A long distance relationship would probably fit nicely into Dylan's egocentric life style.

"I'm guessing it didn't work out with you and your new love," I said in a snippy voice. There was silence on the other end. "Am I right? Hit the nail on the head, did I?"

"You don't have to be so cruel," Dylan replied. "She just wasn't, well, she just wasn't you, Molly. I miss you."

I almost fell for that sugar-coated voice. Then I remembered Dillon was waiting on me downstairs. I wasn't the one who had moved on first. Dylan had made that decision for me and now he wanted me back. Like I was supposed to drop whatever I was doing or whoever I was with and go running to him because it was him. No way. I remembered all those buckets of tears I had cried. Wasted tears. My anger rose.

"I'm sorry things didn't work out for you," I said in my most mature voice. "I have not only moved away, but I have moved on. I suggest you do the same. Enjoy the rest of your summer. I'm going to. Good-bye, Dylan."

As I pulled the phone from my ear, I could hear his voice. It was no longer sugar-coated, but dotted with blasts that would surely warrant bleeps in public. I pushed the END button and the noise stopped. Done.

Sitting on my bed, I pondered how much had changed in only two weeks since leaving California.

I reached for my brush. It was on the floor. That wouldn't normally pique my interest, except it was next to my wallet, my fingernail polish, and my sunglasses which were all the things I kept on my nightstand. The odd part was they were all lined up in a neat straight row. I had not placed them there like that. Frankly, I just wasn't that neat.

Gathering up all the items, I put them back on my nightstand. I stared at them for a moment, trying to figure out how they had ended up on the floor. Maybe I had knocked them off when I was talking to Dylan. But they wouldn't have fallen in such an organized line.

With no rational explanation I dismissed the oddity and headed downstairs to Dillon.

* * *

MOM and Dillon were in the kitchen having smoothies.

"We made one for you," Mom said, as she handed me a tall glass filled with peach colored heaven. "Dillon was just telling me about his basketball camp in Ohio next week."

Great, remind me again that he would be gone for almost a whole week. I sipped on the straw drinking in the sweetness.

"Well, how did your phone call go?" Dillon asked. "I gathered from the conversation it was that other Dylan."

I took a slow sip from my smoothie. "Let's put it this way. I don't think I'll be hearing from him again anytime soon."

Dillon smiled.

Mom slipped off the bar stool. "I think this is my cue to get busy somewhere else. I have a ton of things to do around here and they won't happen by themselves."

Mom always knew when to make herself scarce. That was just one of her many great traits. She also put up with Dad's weird office hours and business trips. Hopefully, he wouldn't have to be gone as often anymore, being in the Midwest instead of at the opposite end of the country from New York. Maybe we could host our own weekend barbeques instead of going to other peoples parties.

The sun was beginning to go down behind the row of oaks lining the driveway.

"Well, I really do need to get going," Dillon said with a hint of reluctance. "I'm meeting a couple of guys who are going to camp with me. We have an early bus to catch in Indianapolis tomorrow morning."

I didn't want him to go, mainly because I wasn't going to see him for nearly a week. But I was also a little stressed over all the new weirdness in this house. I grabbed his hand and held it tightly.

"Hey," Dillon said, squeezing my hand. "I'll be back before you know it. Your mom can use your help this week. I'm sure you girls can find a day to drive to Indianapolis and shop your little hearts out."

"It's not that. I mean, yes, I'll miss you, but all the things we uncovered in the last two days has me a bit on edge. Not that I'm admitting to believing in ghosts. It's just that, well, some of my things were scattered on the floor just now and I didn't put them there."

"Really?" Dillon gave a wicked grin. "Have you looked at the rest of your room? You're not exactly Miss Neatness."

Okay, he was right about my lack of neatness, but that was not everything afoot.

"Last night during my bath," I explained and hoped he would not think I was crazy, "I thought I heard a voice in my bedroom. When I checked it out, I found my stereo on. Then when I was almost asleep, I heard a door creaking. Explain that."

"What's to explain? You must have left the stereo on. Did you have it on before you went into the bathroom and just forget to turn it off?"

"I had it on, but I couldn't find a station with any acceptable music, so I turned it off. I'm sure I turned it off."

"See? Just forgetfulness."

"And the door creaking?" I asked.

"I'm sure some of the doors might slide open due to crooked walls or uneven floors." Dillon was obviously scraping for answers. "Anything else?"

"Well, yes, actually. The first time I was here, before we came to the B&B, I thought I saw a girl's face in the middle window of my room as we were leaving. Explain that."

"Molly, listen to yourself," Dillon pleaded. "You're trying to come up with strange things you think you heard or saw to justify that this house is haunted. It's an old house. Even my house creaks and makes strange noises. Sometimes it has to do with the weather. That's common for older homes. You're going to drive yourself crazy if you continue down this road."

"Maybe you're right," I said trying to convince myself. "I've probably just watched too many horror movies."

"Here's another thing to consider," Dillon added. "I'll bet your realtor didn't tell you that this estate had set empty for thirty-two years. Then about six months ago a crew came in and started renovating it. That could explain the creaking doors. The house is probably settling due to the new construction."

The realtor had most definitely not told us that bit of information and I wondered why. Then I recalled the conversation I had with John on the first day we met. He had seemed very nervous when I peppered him with questions about the history of the estate and its original owners. I had specifically heard him say the last owners had left unexpectedly only a couple of years ago. Thirty-two years wasn't just a couple of years. It was decades.

"John gave us the impression it had only been vacant for a couple of years," I informed Dillon.

"Well, I know for a fact that's not true. No one has lived here in my lifetime. It has been vacant for so long that the ghost stories began surfacing. Some of the kids who were known troublemakers used to come up here and have parties on the porch. They broke windows and painted graffiti on the doors. No one in town thought it would ever be lived in again. It was literally falling down. The roof had holes in it and it was so over grown with vines that you could barely see the house. At one point I thought it had been condemned. The windows were boarded up and some of the entrances were bricked over."

Dillon stopped and an odd look crossed his face.

The same idea must have popped into our heads at the very same instant.

"I wonder why they bricked up the doors?" Dillon asked. "They could have boarded them up like the windows."

Was it to keep something out? Or to keep something in?

Enough had been said tonight to last me for a while. I didn't want to think about creaky doors or distant voices or odd visions. We had no concrete answers, and right now I was more focused on the fact Dillon would be gone for a week.

I walked him to his car, wishing the week was already over.

"You stay out of trouble, Molly Greyson," Dillon ordered in mocking tone.

"Yes, sir," I said with a salute. I was trying to be funny, when inside I was ready to turn on the waterworks. "I'm holding you to your promise about the carnival."

"Officially, I wouldn't miss it for anything." Dillon said.

Flashing that heart-melting grin, he bent over and kissed me on the forehead. Then he climbed in his car, started it, and headed down the winding driveway.

I stayed in that very spot, while he drove off, not moving a muscle for fear the wonderful feeling would evaporate. Then, as if on cue, the first tear rolled down my cheek and dropped on my blouse.

I turned around and looked at the house. It was massive with its stone and brick structure. It was a clear night, and the moon overhead reflected off the copper roof. Overwhelming was an understatement. The house seemed to emerge out of the ground like a monstrous dragon. I focused on the windows of my room. I could see the pink curtains even from the driveway. It was if the dragon had a neat pink bow on her head. I had to giggle a bit at the thought.

Tired, I walked back inside the house. It had been a long day. I was ready for a hot bubble bath and a soft pillow.

Once back in my bedroom, I laid my phone on the nightstand and pulled the chain on the small lamp.

Next to my phone was the card that I had gotten in Las Vegas. I had retrieved it from the box of trash still sitting on my floor.

The card seemed to stare at me, its words giving a silent warning.

CHAPTER 12

THE week went by much quicker than I expected.

I lay across my unmade bed of ruffles, listening to a CD Dillon had given me of a local bluegrass band. It wasn't my kind of music, but it had a definite quality that was beginning to grow on me. And it gave me a moment to think about the last few days.

Mom and I had spent a day in Indianapolis shopping for school clothes. Since Dad's new office was there, we were able to have lunch with him at some fancy restaurant. It was almost like being back in California. Almost. There wasn't an ocean to gaze at while I ate my double chocolate soufflé, but it didn't matter that much to me anymore. And the double chocolate soufflé in Indiana was just as good if not better than that on the west coast.

I had also spent a day with Dillon's mom, helping her at the B&B. She insisted I call her Emily. Mrs. Darby felt too impersonal she had said. I wondered if she treated all of Dillon's girlfriends that well. I wondered if she knew that I considered myself Dillon's girlfriend. It was actually fun assisting guests and meeting new people. She hinted that when Dillon left for college she would be looking for someone to take over his job. She never outright asked, but I think she liked me enough to offer me the job. That was almost a year away. A lot could happen in a year.

With Dillon gone to camp, I tried not to think about crumbling brick walls and creepy basements. I placed the Gypsy's card in the bottom of my jewelry box, so I wouldn't have it falling out of my pocket all the time to remind me of the warning printed on it. I could have thrown it away like Dillon suggested, but for some strange reason I hung on to it.

Out of the blue, Mom walked into my room. "You need a job, Molly," she announced.

"What?" I sputtered, sitting up. "A job? Mom! School starts next week. And there aren't that many places around here to get a job, in case you hadn't noticed."

The only jobs around for someone my age were probably either milking cows or slinging fries at one of the three fast food restaurants.

"I can use an assistant," Mom said with a small smile. "You're a wiz with computers. I just don't have the time to set up new clientele and do all the marketing, too. You can use that over-priced PC for something besides playing games or emailing your friends back in Cali."

All the while she was talking, she was straightening my room, picking things up and moving things around. Why couldn't I have inherited some of her neat-freak trait?

Yeah right, like anyone in California knew I existed anymore. Except Dylan. All he wanted was a convenient long-distance relationship that didn't require much commitment. I had not heard from Robyn or Brianna, or even Alexa. I was sure their mom's weren't asking them to get a job. Their days were filled with sand and ocean and beach parties.

"Well, I wish you'd take the time to call Robyn back," Mom said. "She called me a little while ago and said you hadn't returned her calls. I told her I would tell you. And I really hope you'll think about that assistant job."

Robyn had called? I checked my recent phone log. No calls from Robyn. That was strange. I pushed Robyn's name and heard it begin to ring. When I was about ready to hang up I heard the line click.

"Molly?" Robyn asked, a bit out of breath. "It's about time I heard from you. I have been like burning up your phone."

"I haven't gotten any messages from you," I told her. "I left you a couple of messages during the drive out here. I just thought when you didn't respond that you were mad or something."

"I lost my phone when a huge wave crashed our beach party right after you left," Robyn explained. "I had to get a new phone but Mom wouldn't let me get it right away. She said I needed to be more responsible, so I had to wait an entire week. Do you know how terrible it is to go like even a minute without a phone? Like I thought I'd die."

Yes, I knew exactly how it was to not have the use of a phone. There were places out here that even with my state-of-the-art carrier I didn't have a signal. But I hadn't really thought about it. As a matter of fact, I was hardly on my phone anymore, except to answer a call from Dillon. No one else around here had my number. The only out-of-state call I had received recently was from Dylan and that had been an utter mistake.

"Did you check to make certain you got my number right when you programmed your contacts?" I asked.

"I think I did. Let me check. Hang on." There were beeping sounds from the other end. Then Robyn made a noise of disgust. "Oops. I put in one number wrong. How lame am I? Guess that's the problem."

"I'm sure it was," I replied, trying to sound gracious.

Robyn was still that dizzy blonde I had left back in California.

"So how have you been? Aren't you excited that Dylan is coming to see you next week? What have you been doing way out there in Indiana without a beach?" Robyn fired off question after question, but only one caught my full attention.

"Did you say Dylan is coming to Indiana?" I asked stunned.

"Yes, he said he talked to you. Obviously, he still had your correct number, and he's flying out next week. I bet your heart nearly stopped when you heard the news."

Yes, my heart nearly stopped, but not from talking to him.

"This can't be happening," I said in shock.

"I knew you'd be like over the moon about it," Robyn screeched in her happy voice.

"No, I'm not over the moon," I replied in an angry voice. "I'm not even remotely happy about it."

"What? I thought you'd be thrilled. Don't you miss Dylan?"

"I spoke to Dylan two days after I left," I explained. "He was already with another girl. How do I know that? Because I spoke to her as well. I'm over and done with him. I've moved on."

"Yes, there was another girl, but that was like only for a few days. That's so over. He like really misses you, Molly. He's willing to like give up a few days of the beach to spend with you in the middle of Cornfield County. I'd think you'd be thrilled. Has being in the middle of nowhere like fried your brain? I told the girls Indiana wouldn't be good for you and I was right."

Now the other side of Robyn was coming out. I always knew she could flip her allegiance in a heartbeat, but I never thought it would be on me.

"Dylan and I aren't a couple anymore," I stated as plainly as possible. "He only wants a long-distance relationship with me because I won't be there to see his indiscretions. Besides, I've met someone."

"Molly Greyson, how could you do that to poor Dylan?" Robyn whined.

Poor Dylan? He had never been mistreated in his life. He was the one doing the mistreating, and I was one of his victims. I recalled the vivid memory of his most recent phone call when he blasted me with several colorful adjectives. Well, no more.

"Robyn, you just don't understand. I didn't—"

"Oh no," she interrupted. "I understand perfectly. Just because Dylan had like a little fling you are holding it against him and seeking revenge by hooking up with some hayseed. I don't know you anymore, Molly."

Then the phone went dead.

Wow. That hurt. Robyn, who I thought was my friend, just cut me off without so much as an opportunity to explain what had happened. Was I that shallow? Maybe once, but I had changed. And had I ever used the word 'like' as many times as Robyn did? I was not the same girl I had been in California. I now felt focused, grounded. I had one person to thank for that, and he would be home tomorrow.

I considered calling Robyn back, but quickly changed my mind. She most likely wouldn't answer her phone when she saw the caller ID. Maybe it was best to leave her alone for now. She had made it quite clear that I was no longer her BFF, *best friends forever.*

What if she was telling the truth about Dylan showing up here next week? Surely, he wouldn't be so stupid to fly out here after the way our last conversation had ended. No, I decided, I was not going to let that bother me. I had more important things on my mind.

I ran downstairs and found Mom working out new designs on her sketchpad.

"I think I'll take you up on that offer of being your assistant," I said. "Can we talk salary?"

Mom laughed. "Of course, I'll pay you. Welcome to Greyson's Designs."

That had a nice ring to it. I was glad to see Mom settling in so quickly. She had left several friends to move out here. Hopefully her friends weren't as wishy-washy as mine. John, the realtor, had already shown her a building in downtown Kottersville and one in Indianapolis for her new studio. I wasn't too keen on John, since catching him in a bald face lie about the estate but I hadn't told Mom or Dad yet. I thought I'd let that little scenario play out, and then call him on it at the right moment. I needed more proof, before I let that proverbial cat out of the bag. When Dillon got back, I would have him take me to the records office in Kottersville, so I could do a little research of my own. This was one of those times I really wished I had my driver's license. In Indiana you had to be sixteen and a half before you could get your license. I had turned sixteen just a few weeks before we left California.

Anxious about my first official date with Dillon tomorrow, I thumped up the stairs and headed back into my bedroom.

What was I going to wear? I went through my closet, trying to find the perfect outfit for the carnival. I pulled the chain on the closet light and began to search for a sweater to go with my favorite jeans. There were still a few unpacked boxes stacked at the back of the closet. Dillon and I had gotten preoccupied with the dumbwaiter and never finished unpacking everything.

Just as I reached for the top box, the entire stack came crashing down at me. Startled, I jumped back and let out a yelp, as I saw a figure facing me.

It was just my own reflection in the full length mirror Dillon had placed in front of the little interior closet door.

Nerves on edge, I sat on the closet floor and began going through the first box in search of my pink sweater.

My eyes kept drifting to the back of the closet and the door I knew was behind the mirror. I couldn't stand it any longer. I went to the mirror and pushed it with all my strength. I was able to move it out just enough to see behind it.

The hidden door was standing open about two inches.

Shocked, I stumbled back a couple of steps.

Then I ran to the nightstand and got the skeleton key. I shoved the mirror a little further to the side, so I had just enough room to reach behind it.

With shaking hands, I closed the small door and put the key in the lock. I heard the tumblers click into place.

I shoved the mirror back securely in front of the door and restacked the boxes in front of it. I stood back, watching and listening. Nothing moved. Nothing happened.

Then I remembered what Dillon had said about the recent construction and how the house would have to resettle. Yes, that could explain why the door was standing open.

I grabbed another sweater hanging toward the front of the closet and decided it would do for the carnival tomorrow. No need to go through those boxes tonight, I convinced myself as I pulled the chain on the light and closed the closet door behind me. I decided to ask Dad for a more modern light switch installed in the closet. For some strange reason this one gave me the willies.

After laying my clothes neatly across the chair, I went to pick out matching earrings. As I opened the jewelry box, the Gypsy's card was sitting on top of the earrings I wanted.

I distinctly remembered placing that card in the bottom of the box.

Okay, Molly, keep it together.

I repeated it over and over in my head. Mom must have moved the box, when she was straightening my room earlier. Yes, that must have been it.

My imagination was in overdrive. I turned up the stereo and let a Bluegrass mandolin fill my head.

CHAPTER 13

I woke to a bright and sunny day.

Dillon had sent a text message last night right before bed to let me know he would be leaving Ohio at eight a.m. on a bus bound for Indiana. We had texted once a day, but I hadn't talked to him since he left. He had explained the coaches were pretty strict about any distractions. I was certain that had meant girlfriends. I was just glad to get a text once a day.

Just as I rolled over and reached for my phone, it rang. Startled, I dropped it on the floor.

Hopping out of bed, I reached for the phone and then froze. It was lying face down and next to it was my purse with its contents spilled over the floor. I picked up the phone and checked the ID before answering.

It was Dillon. I pushed accept, while staring at my things scattered across the floor.

"Molly, are you there?" Dillon called, his voice echoing into the room.

"Yes, I'm here," I replied. "I knocked my purse off the nightstand and had to pick up a few things." It was the most likely explanation. I began stuffing items back into my purse. "It's good to hear your voice. Where are you?"

"I'm about four hours away. I should be home by two this afternoon," Dillon said. "I'll be by about four to pick you up for the carnival. That is, if we're still on."

"Of course, why wouldn't we be?"

"Well, I've been gone a week," he said. "I thought you might have forgotten about me."

"Nonsense," I replied. "I vaguely remember something about a date and a carnival with some tall Hoosier boy."

"You're kidding, right?" There was a hint of worry in Dillon's voice.

"Yes, I'm kidding," I said with a laugh. "I've been marking off days on my calendar."

"So, has anything interesting happened while I was gone?" he asked.

I knew he wasn't asking if the corn had tasseled or if I got a new pair of jeans. He wanted to know if anything spooky or strange had taken place. I decided not to tell him about the Gypsy's card or the closet door being unlocked or the contents of my purse being on the floor again.

"Nope, nothing new, except, I got a job."

"A job?" he asked. "Where?"

"I'm going to be my mom's assistant for her design business. I'll be keeping track of all of her contacts and marketing business on the computer. It's right up my alley."

"Good for you," Dillon said with genuine excitement. "I can't wait to see you. Got to go. The bus is ready to leave. See you soon, beautiful."

He called me beautiful.

I fell back on my bed, feeling happy, and stared up at the pink sky of ruffles above me.

Just then I spotted a shadow on the bed canopy above me.

I rolled out of bed and grabbed the chair from my desk. Holding onto one of the bed posters, I stood in the chair. I reached across the fabric canopy and grabbed the object. It was my hairbrush. How had it gotten up there?

I climbed down and shoved the chair back in place. I laid my brush on the nightstand and began to make my bed.

Then I realized there had been something peculiar about my brush. I picked it up and examined it more closely. It had blonde hair in it, curly blonde hair, the total opposite of my long brown hair.

Freaked out, I dropped the brush. It landed on the floor with a soft thump.

I herded the brush into the bathroom using my foot and then maneuvered it with my toes into a plastic baggie. I then picked up the baggie and ran my fingers along the top to seal the evidence. I laid the baggie, containing my brush with someone else's hair in it, inside the linen closet and closed the door.

* * *

AFTER going through just about every article of clothing I had in my closet, I decided on the new jeans I had bought with Mom in Indy and a pink tank top. I added the lightweight pink sweater in case it got chilly. I had already learned that Indiana's weather was unpredictable.

I stood in front of the long mirror at the back of my closet, checking every angle for imperfections. I really didn't like my mirror being in the closet, but I knew why Dillon had moved it in there.

Was the door behind the mirror still locked?

I fought the temptation to sneak a look and pulled the chain on the light. Putting all thoughts of spooky things out of my mind, I headed downstairs and waited for Dillon.

I joined Mom in the main room of the house, where she was going over some of her latest drawings.

"Sit down, Molly," Mom said, looking up from her sketchpad. "You're going to wear a path in the rug pacing like that."

Because this house had so many rooms that could be called great rooms or family rooms, we decided to refer to the place where we spent family time as the main room. It was about the size of a basketball court with a ceiling that reached the height of the second floor.

I checked my phone every five minutes to see if it was four o'clock yet. I don't know why I was so nervous. Dillon was an easy person to be with and I looked forward to seeing him.

Finally, I sat down next to Mom. "So when do I start work?"

"You can start tonight, if you would like."

"Funny, Mom," I grumbled.

"Just kidding," she said with a smile. "The look on your face was priceless. Besides, your dad and I have plans of our own."

At least my parents had each other. I thought about Emily Darby. She was alone, except for Dillon, and he would be leaving for college in less than a year.

Great. Now I was thinking about him leaving for college.

The door chimes sounded.

Startled, I jumped off the sofa. Then raced to the door and pulled it open.

Dillon stood there wearing an Indiana University t-shirt and washed out jeans. His long hair hung slightly across his gorgeous green eyes. I couldn't move. I could barely breathe.

He cleared his throat. "Ready?"

A tiny "yes" was all I could squeeze out.

Mom walked up behind me. "You two have a great time tonight. I hear the carnival is the highlight of the summer around here."

"Yes, it is," Dillon replied. "It's sort of like the official end of summer right before school starts."

It still felt strange to be going back to school in what would be considered the middle of summer in California. But Dorothy wasn't in Kansas anymore. This was my Oz, and it seemed to be getting more and more perfect every day. I didn't need an Emerald City. The wizard here had emerald eyes and they were watching over me.

* * *

THE drive to the fairgrounds took about twenty minutes. The carnival had been set up on the other side of town not too far from the B&B.

"So how was basketball camp?" I asked, making conversation. "Learn any new moves?"

"It was great," Dillon said with excitement. "I met several of the college coaches. I feel good about getting some offers for scholarships."

As happy as I was for him, I knew that meant I would be saying good-bye when those offers rolled in and became reality. Well, it was not going to spoil my night with him. Not that. Not doors that opened by themselves. Not hairbrushes with magically appearing blonde hair. My focus was on Dillon tonight and the possibility of a first kiss.

The multicolored tents of the carnival rose on the horizon. Soon he had the car parked and we were walking among the attractions.

There were rides set up for thrill seekers and plenty of places to get sugar-coated junk food. Almost immediately, I spied the elephant ears stand. We walked around, checking out what each vendor offered.

"Hungry?" Dillon asked, as I stared at the elephant ears passing by me as people enjoyed the cinnamon sugar dough.

"I could eat one of those," I said pointing to the elephant ear.

"Done," he said and dragged me to the stand.

Dillon and I walked around, sharing the elephant ear, our fingers sticky from the sugar.

"Hey!" Dillon shouted. "There's the gang."

Great, I was meeting new people with cinnamon sugar all over me. I wiped my fingers as best as I could on my napkin and made a quick swipe across my mouth.

"Molly, this is Clay, Autumn, Bryan, and Emma," Dillon said, pointing to each one as he called their names. "Everybody, this is Molly."

"Hi," I said with a little wave. "Nice to meet you."

Clay started singing *California Dreamin'*. I felt my cheeks flush.

"Don't embarrass yourself, dude. A singing career isn't in your future," Dillon said. "And I'm not dreaming. California is right here." He grabbed my hand and held it in his.

I blushed even more. My cheeks felt like they were on fire.

Then another girl walked up.

"Well hello, cutie-pie," she said to Dillon. She stood on tiptoes and tried to kiss him.

Dillon backed away, causing her to lose her balance and stumble forward. She stared at me with daggers in her eyes.

"Be nice, Kenzie," Dillon said.

"Is this the California girl everyone is talking about?" Kenzie asked, looking me up and down.

"Come on, Kenzie, lighten up," Clay scolded. "This is Molly. She's new here. Cut her some slack."

"It's pretty plain to see Mr. Darby has moved on," she said, eyeing our coupled hands.

"This isn't the place, Kenzie," Dillon said. "I'm here with Molly. Try to be civil."

"Dillon's right," Emma said. "Don't spoil everybody's evening. Go find Mike. I'm sure you can spoil his evening just fine."

Then Dillon pulled me along, leaving Kenzie to fume.

I was smack dab in the middle of something, but I just didn't know what. Dillon walked away with me in tow, while the other four followed. I turned and looked over my shoulder at Kenzie. She was staring at me and pointing her finger in a silent threat. I turned around quickly. I had plenty of other issues going on in my life and didn't need more.

"What was that all about?" I asked. Then I remembered Dillon had said Kenzie was the name of his last girlfriend. Apparently, it had been an unpleasant break-up. "Never mind. I think I already know the answer."

"Kenzie likes to play games," Dillon explained. "I don't. I'm not a ping pong ball. But in my defense, she's the one who moved on first and then changed her mind. Let's not ruin our night. I've been looking forward to this way too long to allow her to mess it up."

He squeezed my hand. I returned the touch.

It occurred to me that Kenzie was the female version of California Dylan. He was also the one who had moved on first. And he liked to play games. They would make the perfect couple.

"What's going on in that pretty little head of yours?" Dillon asked. "You look like you're up to something."

"Well," I said in a catty voice, "I was just thinking how alike Dylan and Kenzie are. Maybe they should team up."

Dillon gave a deep laugh. "That's just cruel. Wish I'd thought of it."

"Let's go in the spook house," Bryan said. He headed toward a large structure that had crude paintings of ghosts and a zombie standing in front of a spooky house.

I wasn't a fan of these places even back in California. With all the strange things going on at my new house I certainly didn't need to seek out more weirdness. Dillon looked at me with apprehension. I could tell he was worried.

"Come on," Autumn begged. "It will be fun. Besides, none of it's real."

She made a valid point. Zombies were all the rage right now. It might be fun to be scared knowing it wasn't real.

"It's okay," I said, putting on my brave face. "I'll go in. Autumn is right. It's all fake."

"Well, if you're certain it won't upset you," Dillon said, worry in his voice.

"Really, I'll be fine as long as big bad Dillon will promise to protect little old me from the zombies," I said in a little girl voice.

"You know I will," he said in a deep voice. Then he bent down toward my face and I just knew he was about to kiss me.

Just then Clay grabbed Dillon's arm and pulled him toward the spook house entrance.

Rats! Thanks for nothing, Clay!

We followed the rest inside the spook house. It was pitch black. We walked through the darkness until a small light shined ahead of us. It grew larger as we walked. Then the girls screamed and the guys laughed. When we caught up to the rest, the girls were pounding on Bryan and Clay. I looked around the dimly lit room we had entered, but found nothing too scary. The actors must have been regrouping for the next batch of teenage girls behind us. As we rounded a corner, it was pitch black once again. I could feel strings hanging everywhere to mimic walking through spider webs. It was all pretty corny and hokey. Clowns popped out at us, their laughter vibrating through the room in an ear splitting echo. A Gypsy jumped out and grabbed me by the arm just before we reached the exit. I screamed loud and long. Dillon pulled the Gypsy off my arm. I thought he was going to punch him right there.

"Hands off the lady, dude," Dillon ordered, his hand curled in a fist.

The Gypsy actor turned and fled back inside presumably to freak out yet another innocent girl.

Then I saw it. My legs felt like they were tied down with chains. I couldn't raise my arms even to cover my mouth that was open wide and ready to scream. But I couldn't scream. I couldn't move. The heaviness on my chest felt like each breath was going to be my last.

"It's alright, Molly," Dillon said. "That idiot won't bother you again. I have a notion to go to the carnival management and complain."

"What's wrong, Molly?" Clay asked. "You look like you just saw a ghost."

I didn't answer. I couldn't answer. My eyes were riveted on one thing.

"Dillon, what's up with your girlfriend?" Clay asked. "It's just a stupid spook house."

"Molly!" Dillon called, shaking me by the shoulders.

I could clearly hear all the conversation around me. It was as if I were in some sort of time bubble. Even when I felt his arms around my shoulders I still couldn't speak.

Then the magic shroud that encased me released its grip and allowed me to raise my arm. I pointed beyond Dillon's shoulder toward a red box with glass on three sides.

He turned toward a glass box with a mechanical dummy inside it.

I knew exactly what it was. It was a Gypsy fortune teller.

Was it the one from Las Vegas? Had it followed me here?

CHAPTER 14

"YOU guys go on," Dillon told the others. "We'll catch up with you. I think Molly needs a minute."

A minute would be good, but it would even be better if we could just hit the rewind button and avoid the spook house.

"Molly," Dillon said, turning my face toward his. "Are you alright? What has you so upset?"

"The box," I managed in a weak voice. Then I pointed toward the glass box across the room.

Dillon looked confused. "What's wrong with it?"

Without answering, I walked slowly toward the box. People going through the spook house came running around me with their mouths open, but I paid no attention to their garbled screams. I had shut out everything and was focused on the box.

Could this be the same box I saw in Las Vegas? There must be lots of these things floating around the country. I had to make certain it wasn't the same Gypsy.

I felt for Dillon's hand, as he came up behind me. I grabbed it tightly and stopped in front of the box.

The Gypsy was still, her eyes closed and her head bent toward her chest. The worn bandana with the black curls sticking out from beneath it looked the same. I couldn't see her face to tell if she was the same mannequin. Also, the tattered lace of her sleeve covered her right hand, so I couldn't see if the pinkie finger was missing.

I grabbed the box and shook it side-to-side trying to dislodge the material and expose her hand.

"What are you doing Molly?" Dillon whispered, looking around nervously. "We'll get in trouble if we break this machine. Stop it."

The Gypsy's head shook back and forth as the box moved, but the sleeve stayed in place.

"Give me a dollar bill," I said, almost in a panic.

"What? Why?" Dillon looked at me like I had lost my mind.

"Please, just give me a dollar," I begged.

"Okay, okay." Dillon rummaged through his wallet in search of a one dollar bill.

While he was searching, I studied the Gypsy more closely. I needed to see the face with the peeling paint and black eyes.

I took the dollar from Dillon and loaded it into the slot on the side of the box. The Gypsy moved immediately. Her head jerked up and her eyes flashed open. Dillon and I both jumped back, as she began her awkward movements. Her mouth moved, but no sound came from it. Then, as before, she stopped as quickly as she started. Her eyes stared ahead, empty black pools.

"Quick, give me another dollar," I demanded.

Poor Dillon slipped another dollar into my hand, and I shoved it into the slot.

Just like back in Las Vegas, this time the Gypsy moved in a more fluid motion. Her hands rose from the crossed position and the lacy sleeve fell back exposing her fingers.

"No!" I shouted. "It can't be! It's not possible!"

"Calm down, Molly," Dillon pleaded. "What's not possible?"

The pinkie finger was missing on her right hand. She was the same Gypsy that had produced the card with the strange warning on it.

A demented smile crossed her puppet-like peeling face. Then a card shot out, hitting the ground at our feet.

Dillon reached down and picked up the card. Without reading it he looked at me.

Shaking, I pulled the first card out of my purse and held it out to Dillon.

"I thought you threw that away," he said.

"I tried several times, but something kept telling me to keep it," I said. "Now I have two cards."

Dillon flipped the new card over and silently read it.

"Well, what does it say?" I asked. "Tell me."

He hesitated and tossed me a worried look.

I grabbed the card from his hand and read it silently: *You have arrived at journeys end. The once living has awakened. The ghosts of lost souls surround you. Beware, Molly.*

"I don't know what's going on," Dillon said pushing me away from the box, "but I do know we need to get out of here."

As we walked away, I turned around. I gripped Dillon's arm, my fingernails digging deep. He turned around in pain.

The Gypsy's face had dark lines running down her cheeks. It was as if she were crying black tears. The paint around her eyes had turned to liquid. One last electrical jolt passed through her ancient internal gears and her head hung down in rest upon her chest.

The Gypsy was still once again.

* * *

ONCE outside the spook house, neither of us looked back.

The gang stood by the Ferris wheel, waving us toward them.

Dillon ignored them. He grabbed my arm and did not stop until we were on the other side of the Tilt-a-Whirl.

"Okay," Dillon said, catching his breath. "What's going on? Don't leave out any details."

I began my story about the trip across country and our first stop in Las Vegas. I explained that I saw the box by sheer accident and what happened when I put dollar bills into it. Just like this time, the Gypsy had produced a card with a warning specifically for me.

"I don't know what possessed me to keep the card," I admitted. "It was like voodoo. It seemed to have a spell over me. Just when I was beginning to think it a hoax of some kind, I ran into the very same Gypsy at a gas station as we were leaving Las Vegas. Now she turns up here in a small time carnival. That's just not a coincidence."

"Are you absolutely certain it's the same Gypsy?" he asked. "There were probably hundreds of those boxes produced and many are probably still in circulation around the country."

"I know. I thought the same thing. But when I saw that the little finger on her right hand was missing, I was certain. Now I have another card to add to my collection." I held up the two cards, side-by-side. "This machine cannot be directing her warnings at more than one Molly. And don't forget, she used my full name on the first card."

"Maybe this time it's a warning for you to let go of the fascination you have with bricked up doors and ghost hunts," Dillon said.

I reread the cards. "The first card says my journey will end where the once living still tread. The second card says I am at journey's end. Okay, so she meant I'd end up here." I continued to compare the cards. "The first card warns me to steer clear of visions. The second card says the once living has awakened. Could it possibly be referring to the vision I saw of the girl in my window?"

"You mean the vision you thought you saw," Dillon corrected. He was obviously looking for a simple answer.

"It could have been my mind playing tricks on me because of the old photographs I saw in the ballroom," I admitted. "I haven't seen anything since. Well, at least not the vision of a figure." I looked at the cards again. "It says the visions are the ghosts of lost souls on the first card. The second card says they now surround me. Both say to beware. These cards are in sequence."

"Do you think she was trying to warn you to not get involved? Afraid you'll open a can of worms?" A serious expression crossed Dillon's face. "Dead worms."

"Maybe, but it's too late now." I thought about bricked up doors and unexplainable happenings. "Or maybe the Gypsy was sending a message not to stop me, but to encourage me."

"A message about what?" Dillon asked. "She isn't real. She's just an old doll in a glass box."

With that, he herded me away from the carnival and back to his car.

"I'm taking you home," he said, opening the car door.

I didn't argue.

* * *

DILLON pulled his car into the driveway of my new monster house.

I jumped out before he could open my door, and continued the conversation that had been ongoing during the twenty-minute drive.

"I disagree," I argued. "I think the Gypsy, or someone, knew I was coming here and wants me, wants us, to dig into the mystery behind the bricked up door and odd happenings. I think she wants us to uncover whatever has stirred up the lost souls and help put them to rest."

"I don't know, Molly," Dillon said, scratching his head. "That's really digging deep for an explanation. What makes you think the warning includes me?"

"Because, Dillon," I said, more certain of myself by the minute, "you have a bricked up door, too. It's time to find out what's behind all these doors. The Gypsy didn't say 'don't go looking for ghosts'. She said 'beware'. And if I remember my dictionary well enough, beware means to take heed or be cautious. It doesn't mean don't do something."

"Your mind is made up isn't it?" Dillon gave a weary sigh. "There's nothing I can do to persuade you to change it, is there?"

"Nope. I'm afraid not. It looks like we'll be going to Kottersville Town Hall first thing Monday morning. We have some ghosts to find."

I had been so absorbed in our conversation about the Gypsy I had lost track of my surroundings. I realized we were standing on the steps to my house. Dillon was a step below me making our height nearly even.

Just then Dillon kissed me on the lips.

"Wow," I said, opening my eyes. "Our very first kiss."

"You are something else, Miss Molly Greyson," Dillon said, flashing a wicked grin at me. "Go to bed and get some rest. Don't do anymore ghost hunting tonight. Promise?"

"I promise," I said, closing the front door behind me.

After I saw his car taillights disappear down the winding driveway, I bounded up the stairs.

When I got to my room, I placed the second card from the Gypsy into my jewelry box alongside the first card.

Somehow I wasn't frightened by the thought of ghost hunting. That first kiss was enough to convince me I had a partner to help me solve the mystery.

The first thing I needed to do in the morning was study the old photos hanging on the walls of the ballroom. I would start with the one of the girl with the curly blonde hair.

CHAPTER 15

AMAZINGLY, I had slept like a baby.

The first thing that entered my mind upon waking was that kiss. It played over and over in my head. I swooned. I had never swooned over California Dylan, but ever since arriving in Indiana I had done a lot of swooning.

The second thing that entered my mind was the ballroom. I pulled on some old clothes knowing Dillon wouldn't be by until later. I skipped breakfast and headed to the ballroom.

The double stained-glass doors to the ballroom creaked softly, as I pushed them open. The sun shone through tall windows. I walked around the room, studying photos that hung in huge wooden frames with elaborate carved designs. Some frames were painted with gold paint that was peeling and flaking off onto the floor. There were old photos of the original family, the Kotter's, and newer photos of people wearing more modern clothing. Well, clothing newer than the late nineteenth century.

One photo was of a young girl with curly blonde hair. She looked sort of—well, distant, with a blank expression. She had an undeniable look of distraction. In many of the older photos the people were serious, not smiling, and looking right at the camera. But in the girl's photo she wasn't looking at the camera. Her eyes looked to the far right. It seemed that was the last photo taken of that group of people. The next photo on the wall was with a different family from an entirely different decade.

There seemed to be a span of time between some photos, like a decade or so had passed given the difference in the style of clothing. I wondered why there were such obvious gaps in time. With Dillon's help tomorrow, I hoped to be able to learn more about the history of the house. The Town Hall should have records of the names and dates of past owners. School started in three days, and I wanted some answers before that.

I went back to the photo with the girl. I blew at the dust covering the glass. In the lower right hand corner there seemed to be some writing. I looked around for a rag or something to wipe away accumulated dirt. Finding nothing, I spit on my finger and rubbed away the dirt. In fancy script the plaque read: *Circa 1885 – Birthday Party.*

This was possibly a photo of the Kotter family celebrating a birthday. But was the girl a part of the family celebration or one of the guests? Whose birthday were they celebrating? In the photo there was an older woman seated between two couples. The couple on the left was very young, holding a baby, and the girl with the curly blonde hair was standing with the other couple. That meant if the house was built in 1876 by Benjamin Kotter, then he would have lived here almost ten years when this photo was taken. I needed to know if this was the Kotter family and why Benjamin Kotter wasn't in the photo unless, he was possibly the one taking the photo.

I heard a voice that sounded like my mom but it was distant, muffled. I looked around but there wasn't anyone else in the room with me.

"Where are you, Molly?" the voice asked.

"I'm in the ballroom," I answered, my voice echoing across the chamber.

A cold feeling swept through me. If that wasn't Mom calling me, then who was it? Or did I just imaging the voice?

It felt like the eyes in every photo in the room were fixed on me.

I rushed to the door and ran right into Mom.

"What's wrong, Molly?" Mom asked. "Did I scare you?"

"I thought I heard someone call my name," I replied, a little rattled.

Mom laughed. "That was me. I found an old intercom box in our bedroom. I tracked it down and realized this house is equipped with an intercom system. There must be a box in here if you heard my voice. Isn't that awesome?"

I looked around the ballroom. I didn't know what an intercom box looked like, but I knew there had to be one in here.

"So what are we looking for exactly?" I asked.

"Well, I found the one in our room behind a painting," Mom said. "It's a small bronze box about six inches square with buttons. It was like someone was purposely trying to cover it up."

I went directly to the photo of the Kotter family. This was the last place I was standing when I heard Mom's voice. I pulled carefully at the photo. It wasn't hung like a normal frame from a hook, but was mounted on hinges that allowed the photo to swing open like a door. Behind it was a square bronze box with buttons just as Mom had described.

We looked at each other and smiled in victory.

"I'm really glad to have an intercom system," Mom said, looking quite pleased. "This place is so huge. An intercom will save me a lot of time looking for you. I thought for a minute I was going stir crazy in this big old house."

"Why would you say that?"

"I had heard voices and thought I might be imagining them," Mom answered with a shrug. "But now I know where they were coming from. I'm certain there's a box in your room, because I heard you singing this morning."

I had not been singing this morning. It was no secret that I couldn't sing a tune if I tried.

"Oh, really," I stammered. "Well, it's good to know that we can keep in touch, even from three floors away." I offered a weak smile. "How did you know it was coming from my room?"

"Well, I just assumed you were in your room," Mom explained, "since you're the only one with a sweet girly voice in this house."

I had been in the ballroom for at least an hour. If she heard the singing during that time, then it definitely was not me.

"I see you're in here inspecting these old photos," Mom said, looking around. "I seem to remember John said there used to be several trunks of old photos and memorabilia in the basement. If you're interested."

Butterflies fluttered in my stomach at the very thought of the basement, but the idea of finding more photos was very tempting. Of course, I would wait until Dillon came before venturing into the basement. First, I needed to see if my room had an intercom box.

Mom went down to the kitchen to prepare some sandwiches for a late lunch. She knew Dillon was coming over, and she loved to entertain. It was Sunday, but Dad was doing some work from home today. Mom expected Dillon and me to have lunch with them on the screened porch. Since I had skipped breakfast, it sounded good to me.

I went back up to my room and started searching the walls. There were only two paintings in my room. I looked behind the first painting. Nothing. I looked behind the second painting and was surprised to find nothing there, as well. Odd.

Then I remembered that the wallpaper in the bathroom had hidden the dumbwaiter door. Maybe the wallpaper in the bedroom was hiding an intercom box. I knew Mom had plans to tear out that unsightly paper and replace it, so if I destroyed it there shouldn't be a problem.

I ran my hands along the walls, feeling every bump. Next to the closet door, I felt what could be an intercom box beneath the paper.

I went into the bathroom to get my nail file and found my make-up bag spilled out on the floor. I must have knocked it off in my hurry to get to the ballroom this morning. I picked up everything and put it back in my bag, everything except my mascara. It was missing. I searched under the vanity and across the floor, but no mascara.

With nail file in hand, I returned to the spot near the closet door and ran my fingers around the shape under the paper. I punctured the paper and began to run my file along the imaginary border. The old and stiff paper tore open like tissue and revealed an intercom box.

It was right next to the closet door, which had a door in the back of it that was bricked up with who knows what behind it.

A cold shiver ran up my spine.

I had a pretty good idea where the singing had come from.

* * *

AT two o'clock the door chimes rang.

I raced to the door and slid across the polished wood floors. It was Dillon.

"Mom has lunch ready for us," I said, dragging him by the hand to the screened porch where Mom and Dad sat, enjoying the summer afternoon. "Then I have some interesting news."

"Can't you just tell me now?" Dillon asked.

"Nope, I want to eat first. I skipped breakfast and we're going to need some energy if I'm right about this."

"Okay, whatever you say, boss," Dillon said in a jovial tone.

He flashed that famous grin. Once again I felt a swoon coming on.

We ate lunch quickly and made small talk with my parents. Dillon was still chewing his last bite, when I excused us. I told Mom I had some furniture I wanted to switch in my room and Dillon was going to use his muscle to help get the job done. She tossed me an odd look and then just smiled.

"What's the big secret?" Dillon asked, as we climbed the stairs to my room.

"Just wait." I pulled him into my room, and then herded him over to the closet. "See? This is an intercom box. We have an intercom system in this house."

"Okay," he said, looking quite unimpressed. "Lots of houses have intercom systems. My house has one."

That was a surprise me. "You never mentioned that."

"Didn't seem relevant," he said with a shrug. "What's so special about *your* intercom system?"

"I was in the ballroom this morning," I explained, "and Mom called me over the intercom. The one I didn't know anything about until this morning. Anyway, it startled me, and she said there was probably one in every room in the house."

"And your point?" he asked, looking confused.

"I found this box in my room. Don't you see? It's right next to my closet door." I stood there waiting for him to make the connection.

"I still don't know what this box has to do with your closet," Dillon said a bit dumbfounded.

I didn't want to tell him Mom was hearing voices, too, but he left me no choice, since he obviously wasn't putting two and two together.

"Mom said she heard me singing in my room this morning," I said.

"And that is supposed to mean something?"

"Dillon, I wasn't singing in my room this morning," I stated point-blank.

Dillon's mouth dropped open. Now he was getting it. "You weren't singing in your room? Then who? What?"

"Mom also made the comment now she knows where the voices are coming from," I added. "She linked them to the intercom system. Don't you get it? Mom is hearing voices, too, only she doesn't realize they aren't mine or Dad's voices she's hearing."

"So your Mom is hearing voices. Have you heard anymore voices since your first night here?"

"No," I answered, "but things are messed up or missing in my room every day. There is always something spilled across the floor. And then there's the hairbrush."

Dillon still looked unconvinced. "I have an idea how things get on your floor, Miss Not-so-neat, but what's this about a hairbrush?"

"I found my hairbrush on top of my canopy," I explained. "Don't you see? This box is right outside my closet. The door inside my closet is bricked up for a reason. I don't think it's a coincidence that Mom heard a voice coming from my room."

Dillon still seemed perplexed. "But how did she know the singing was coming from your room?"

"She thinks I'm the only girl in this house," I said quietly.

"But you are the only other girl in this house," Dillon said.

"Am I?"

CHAPTER 16

IT was all out in the open now.

Dillon knew that I believed there were ghosts in this house. But did he believe it, too?

"So, what are your thoughts?" I asked, waiting for some kind of reaction from him.

"Let me see the hairbrush," Dillon said.

I went into the bathroom and retrieved the baggie that held the evidence. I handed it to Dillon and he opened it carefully.

"Don't touch it," I said quickly. "I don't want any extra fingerprints on it. Just in case."

"In case of what?" Dillon pulled the brush out of the bag. "Do you really think ghosts leave fingerprints?"

It did sound silly when said out loud, but I still didn't want anyone else to touch it. Just in case.

"What is your take on the curly blonde hair?" he asked. "You must have some idea in that crazy little head of yours as to how it got there."

"I do," I said. "But I can't explain it. I have to show you."

Grabbing Dillon by the hand, I dragged him down to the ballroom. It was time he met the girl with the curly blonde hair who had me so mesmerized.

I stood in front of the photo that captivated me and pointed.

Dillon studied the picture for a moment. "Is this the girl?"

"Yes. See how she's looking to the right, away from the camera?"

"Not only that," Dillon said, "but she looks freaked out."

"Exactly!" I blurted. "Her focus is to the right, like she's afraid of something that no one else seems to see." Finally, Dillon and I were on the same page. "Did you also notice that the photo seems to have been taken in this very corner of the ballroom? It's almost precisely where we're standing."

Dillon took a couple steps backward. Then he turned, facing the same direction that the family was facing in the photo. He looked to the right just as the girl had in the photo.

"What are you doing?" I asked.

"I'm trying to fix on the direction the girl was looking," he explained. "To see what might have drawn her attention."

We both looked to the far wall. The only thing on it was a large tapestry.

Dillon walked toward the tapestry and tried to push it to the side. It was old and very heavy. He looked around for something to help him move it. He pulled a chair across the floor and stood on it reaching up to unhook the massive woven rug from its position on the wall. With much straining and several grunting noises, the tapestry fell to the floor with a poof of dust. Its golden ropes and tassels coiled on top, like a pile of snakes.

I gasped, when I saw what the tapestry had been covering.

It was an accordion type metal door. Inspecting it closer, we realized it was an old elevator. Not only did this house have dumbwaiters and an intercom system, but it also had its very own elevator. Would wonders never cease?

"Why didn't John say something about all this stuff?" I asked. "Elevators? Dumbwaiters? Intercoms? Did he think we would change our minds and not move in if we knew?"

"I don't know why John has been so secretive, but I'm with you on this one," Dillon said. "It seems someone has gone to great lengths to cover up these things. We need to investigate the people who lived here." Dillon pushed open the elevator gate. "Want to take a ride?"

"No thanks," I replied. "I'm not getting into an elevator without knowing where I will end up."

Dillon closed the door and took a step back. "It probably stops on every floor and could possibly go down to the basement."

"Speaking of the basement," I said, swallowing hard, "Mom said John told her there might be more photos down there."

"I guess there's only one way to find out if John was telling the truth this time." Dillon went around the room, inspecting the rest of the pictures on the walls. "Are there any other photos of the girl?"

"The only one that I could find is here," I said pointing to a photo.

"Wow, she's a lot younger in this one," Dillon said, looking closely at the photo. "But there's still something creepy about her. Do you have any clue as to who she might be?"

I went back to the first photo and showed Dillon the inscription. "No, not really, but I assume it must be the Kotter family. I guess we'll just have to find out when we go to the Town Hall tomorrow."

"Or," Dillon offered, "we can go down in the basement and search through those alleged photos for some answers right now."

Great. Not exactly what I had in mind for a Sunday afternoon.

* * *

WE decided to take the back stairs, hoping to avoid Mom and Dad.

I didn't want to alarm Mom with the notion of ghosts, until I was certain we had enough evidence, especially since she had already heard voices. The old intercom system garbled voices so much it was difficult to know exactly who was talking.

The basement wasn't any more appealing this time than it had been the first time we went down there. I decided to stay away from the large opening in the back. When we were down there before, we had not inspected any of the rooms. At the time I had only wanted to find my toilet paper on the dumbwaiter and leave. Maybe this time I would remember to take the toilet paper with me.

Dillon had no problem with the door of the first room, as he shined his flashlight ahead. There were a few boxes inside that were overflowing with old canning jars. The door to the second room had a broken knob, but Dillon managed to get it open. Inside was a rusty metal bed frame and what looked like the remains of a dirty mattress rotting from old age. I wondered if it was just stored down here or if someone had actually slept there. The room felt like a prison cell. A cold chill ran up my spine at the thought.

The third and last room was locked.

"Key?" Dillon asked.

I shook my head indicating I didn't have it with me.

"Stand back," Dillon said.

After taking a step back, he kicked the door just below the lock. With a cracking sound, the door popped open. On the other side was a small chamber with a dirt-encrusted window. Dillon reached up and pulled a cord hanging from the ceiling. A weak bulb hissed to life, casting dim light through the room. To one side sat three big trunks, like those used when traveling on a ship.

"Bingo," Dillon said, as he headed to the first trunk.

"Wait." I wasn't certain I wanted to see what was inside. "What if there are things we shouldn't be messing with in these trunks? What if we stir up evil spirits or something?"

"Really, Molly," Dillon chided. "Now you're worried about evil spirits? Yesterday you said you didn't believe in ghosts."

Was he making fun of me?

"Besides, your mom said there were just old photos down here," Dillon added. "She didn't mention any evil spirits lurking around."

Okay, now he *was* making fun of me.

I stood straight and tried to look brave, even though I could feel my knees shaking. "Alright, wise guy, open it up."

Dillon had a little trouble with the rusty latch, but managed to push the lid open. Dust flew everywhere. Between sneezes I was able to see what looked like stacks of framed photos. It was like they had been taken directly off a wall and placed inside.

"This is strange," Dillon said, as he picked up the first photo.

"What's strange?" I asked, straining to see the photo.

"Look. There's no dust on this glass." Dillon ran his hand over the face of the photo. "With all this dust down here, there should be at least some on this glass, but there's not."

I examined the glass. Dillon was right. No dust. I looked at the other photos in the trunk. They were all the same, clean and dust free.

"Okay," I said, "someone is playing a trick on us. How can these photos be this clean in such a dirty trunk?"

"I'd say someone recently removed them," Dillon offered. "Then hid them here, thinking no one would find them."

"Why? They don't seem to be anything special." I examined more of the photos. "This doesn't make sense. These pictures aren't in any particular order. They seem to be random photos from different decades. They're not even of the same people."

Dillon went over and worked on the second trunk. This time he had to use his pocket knife to force open the latch. There were no framed photos in this trunk. Instead, it was full of loose photos in all sizes and shapes covered in a blanket of dust. He sat down on the floor beside the trunk and grabbed the first photo.

I picked up the next photo and carefully brushed dust away from the face. It was a photo of a man who appeared to be very old. His clothing hinted the photo could have been from the early nineteen hundreds.

"Do you think this could be Benjamin Kotter?" I asked.

"Possibly. Who knows." He flipped over a couple of photos and then dug deeper in the trunk. "There aren't any dates on the backs."

Feeling brave, I walked over to the third trunk. It was much larger than the other two. I flipped open the latch without any problem. To my amazement, this trunk was filled with clothing. I pulled out the first item. It was an old animal skin stole of some sort. It even had the head of the animal still attached. I quickly tossed it to the floor, disgusted anyone would do that to an animal and have the nerve to wear it. Then I found a beautiful purple satin dress. The lace around the neckline was yellow and ragged. When new, it must have been an elegant gown.

I held up the gown in front of me and turned to Dillon. "How do I look?"

"Very nice," he replied. "It looks like it might even fit you."

He continued to sort through the photos. Then he stopped and held one photo up to the light for a better view.

"No, this must be a mistake," he said with a puzzled look.

"Let me see," I said.

I took the cracked and faded photo from his hand. It was the girl with the curly blonde hair. She was older, and she was wearing the same dress I was holding in my hands.

Dillon took the photo from me and flipped it over. His face turned white as chalk. Then he held out the back for me to see.

"Molly Greyson," I read aloud.

The room began to spin.

I dropped the dress to the floor and fell to my knees.

CHAPTER 17

AWAKING in a cloudy haze, I found myself on the floor of the musty basement and cradled in Dillon's arms.

"Finally," Dillon said, stroking my hair. "You're back. For a minute I was afraid I was going to have to call 911."

"What happened?" I tried to sit up, but my head throbbed and the room began to sway. Then I spied the photo on the floor next to me and I remembered.

I reached for the photo, but Dillon grabbed my arm.

"I need to see this again," I pleaded.

He released his grip, and I picked up the photo. My hands shook, as I flipped it over to see the words.

"What's going on?" I asked. "How can my name be on this photo?"

Dillon was silent for a moment, as if struggling for a response. "Somehow her name and your name are the same."

"But how can that be? This can't be a coincidence. There must be a logical explanation."

"Is there any way you might be related?" Dillon asked.

"What?" I found the idea more than a little unnerving. "Related to this girl? That's crazy. I don't know of any relatives from this area."

"Have you or anyone in your family ever done genealogy work on your family history?"

"I don't know," I replied, a bit unsure. "There must be some other explanation. Unless—" I pulled the Gypsy's cards from my pocket. "Unless the wording on the first card was wrong and it was supposed to read 'Beware *of* Molly Greyson'. Do you think the Gypsy was trying to warn me about this girl who just happened to have my name?"

Dillon looked skeptical. "You do realize what you're saying, right?"

"I know exactly what I'm saying," I replied with conviction. "The Gypsy was warning me about a ghost with the same name. And, yes, before you even ask I do believe in ghosts now."

"So where do we go from here?" Dillon asked.

It was the right question to ask. I paused for a moment and thought about it. "Do you believe in ghosts? Are we on the same page here? If not, tell me now. I'll do the research on my own."

"It does seem that you and this girl—this ghost have some kind of connection." He paused, taking a deep breath. "But I'm not sure about the Gypsy's part in this."

"Did you not read the card?" I asked in frustration. "The Gypsy was the first one to send me a warning about this ghost. How in the world could that mechanical dummy spit out a card with my name on it without there being some connection here? Don't ask me to explain it, because I can't. But my instincts tell me to take the card seriously."

"Don't get all mad," Dillon said, putting his arms around my shoulders and pulling me to him. "I'll help you get to the bottom of this." Then he released me and kissed my forehead. "Are you ready to get out of this dingy basement?"

"Not on your life." I dropped to my knees and started to dig through the photos in the trunk.

"I thought you hated basements," Dillon said. "I thought you'd be glad to get out of here."

"I need to see if there are more photos of the girl. Of Molly." As the words came out of my mouth, they felt strange. Never in my wildest dreams could I have imagined someone else with my same name. And to think she had lived in this very house. It was not a coincidence, and I intended to prove it.

We spent the next hour going over all of the photos we could find, but there were no more of Molly. It was as if we were meant to find the only one in the trunk. We did find photos of what I assumed were other family members, but she wasn't with them. She was only in the one photo with her family that still hung on the wall in the ballroom.

"I guess our work is done," Dillon said, placing the photos back in the trunk. "There's really nothing more we can do down here today."

Nodding in agreement, I picked up the photo of Molly. Then I reached down and picked up the purple dress.

"Are you certain you want to take that with you?" Dillon asked, pointing to the dress.

"I am," I replied, folding the dress over my arm. "Maybe she will come back to get it."

* * *

DILLON didn't hang around late.

He hesitated near the front door. "Are you certain you're going to be okay? Maybe you should sleep in one of the bedrooms on the second floor. Closer to your parents."

"I'll be fine. I'm so exhausted I could sleep sitting up." I tried to be as convincing as possible, so he wouldn't worry. I just had not quite convinced myself. "You have to get some rest, too. We have a busy day ahead of us tomorrow."

"Keep your phone charged and by your side just in case. Call me at any hour." Dillon just stood there, looking at me and holding my hand. "Maybe I should stay here tonight. I could sleep in a spare bedroom."

"Really?" I found the idea of having Dillon sleep just one floor below thrilling, but knew it was not practical. Mom and Dad would ask a ton of questions about why he needed to sleep over when he only lived on the other side of a very small town. And I was not ready to tell them what was going on. I needed more proof. I did feel optimistic about what we would find tomorrow in the town archives. "Go home. I'll be fine."

Dillon grabbed my phone and checked the charge on its battery. "See? It's only twenty-five percent. You need to plug this in as soon as you get to your room. Put it under your pillow."

I could tell that he was stalling.

"Yes sir," I replied and gave him a mock salute.

"This is not funny. This is serious stuff."

I opened the front door and with both hands shoved Dillon over the threshold.

"Good night. I'll see you bright and early." I flashed him my best smile and put a hint of flirtation on it.

That must have convinced him, because he bent down and kissed me on the lips. Although this time it was more of a concerned kiss than a passionate one. Now he had my attention.

"Don't worry," I said. "Now get out of here."

With a wink, I closed the door.

I turned to head up the stairs. Mom and Dad were in their room. When I reached the second floor, I considered checking out one of the guest bedrooms but decided against it. I would not give in to fear.

I climbed the last set of stairs to my circular bedroom. Before opening my door, I looked down the long hallway toward the ballroom. The lights on the walls gave a warm amber glow, casting shadows off the furniture in the hall. I noticed a more bright light coming from the ballroom through the etched glass doors.

Against my better judgment, I headed toward the ballroom to check it out.

When I opened the glass doors, I saw light coming from the crystal chandelier hanging in the middle of the room. Had Dillon turned it on earlier to see what the chandelier looked like when lit? Had Mom or Dad been up here?

I pushed the lower button on the ancient light switch and the light went out. I made a mental note to remind Dad to get an electrician in here to update these old switches.

Moonlight shined through the windows and bounced off the crystals on the chandelier. It cast a rainbow effect across the room and onto the photo of Molly and those I assumed to be her family. As the multiple colors crossed Molly's face, it seemed as though her expression changed. It now looked more like desperation rather than fear.

Nonsense. I was letting my mind play tricks on me, and the lighting wasn't helping.

I closed the ballroom door behind me and walked back to my bedroom, ready for a hot bath and a good night's sleep.

When I got to my bedroom, I looked around and took note of everything. Nothing seemed out of place. No items were lined up on the floor in orderly fashion.

I tossed the purple dress onto my desk and headed for that well deserved hot bath.

Adding chamomile-vanilla bubble bath to the water, I tried to soak away my stress. The water was hot, making sweat beads gather on my forehead. I closed my eyes and laid my head back on my tub pillow. *Ahhhh*. All I needed now was the music player I had left on the desk. But the quiet was also nice.

A small squeak jarred me from my Zen place.

My eyes popped open. I sat up quickly, causing water and bubbles to splash out onto the floor.

I looked at the bathroom door. It was still closed. I looked around the over-sized bathroom.

At first, I didn't see anything out of place. Then I noticed that the mirror was clouded with condensation.

The words *HELP ME* were printed on that steamy mask.

I jumped out of the tub and grabbed for my robe. Skidding on a film of soap bubbles, my feet flew out from under me. My cheek hit the vanity, as I slid across the tile floor. I ended up flat on my back, staring up at the dumbwaiter door.

Gathering my strength, I scrambled on all fours away from the dumbwaiter. I reached the large shag rug in the center of the room and sat with my knees under my chin, arms wrapped tightly around my legs.

The air in the bathroom had turned icy cold. I sat there, shivering.

What did the words mean? Was it Molly? Was she trying to tell me she was in some sort of danger? Could a ghost even be in danger?

Somehow I didn't feel like I was alone anymore. The room was still steamy, but the air felt cold.

After a few minutes to catch my breath, I managed to stand. A bit wobbly, I shuffled across the soapy floor to the mirror.

It was a large mirror that spanned the width of the vanity. To the right of the words I wiped clear a space just large enough to see my face. A bruise was already forming in shades of purple and blue on my right cheek. This was going to be hard to explain.

I left the words on the mirror, hoping to show them to Dillon tomorrow. Maybe they would not fade away completely overnight.

Crossing the shag rug, I pulled my pajamas off a hook on the inside of the bathroom door. The cold spot was gone. I felt alone.

I left the bathroom door open just enough to let my lava lamp night light cast a sparkling beam across the bed. I climbed into bed and reached for my phone charger. I plugged my phone in per Dillon's request and started to press the switch on the table lamp.

It was then that I saw the purple dress. No longer crumpled on the desk, it was now spread out neatly over the back of the desk chair, as if ready to be worn the next day.

I was right. Molly had come back for her dress.

CHAPTER 18

THE alarm on my phone vibrated under my pillow like an earthquake, shaking me awake.

I flipped over and saw the purple dress was still laid out neatly on the desk.

I staggered to the bathroom, rubbing my eyes and stretching.

The mirror was clear. The words HELP ME had vanished.

Great. Now Dillon wouldn't believe me.

Then I realized I had actually gotten some sleep. I had not stayed up worrying over the possibility of a ghost being in the same room with me.

Oddly enough, I wasn't even afraid. I didn't feel an evil presence. I sensed she needed my help. I didn't know how or if I could help Molly, but I was going to put all my effort into trying.

And Mr. Dillon Darby was going to assist.

* * *

DILLON entered unannounced through the mud room door.

I was sitting in the kitchen, eating a bagel with strawberry cream cheese and talking to Tilly.

Mom had hired Tilly on a temporary basis right after we moved in just to help with arranging furniture and cleaning up empty rooms. Tilly was a wiz in the kitchen and Mom, bless her heart, had unresolved issues with the oven. Tilly could whip up a meal from almost nothing and make it taste like a five star restaurant. I could tell that Mom loved the idea of having an assistant in the house. She would never use the term maid, because she wanted Tilly to feel like part of the family. Although I was also Mom's assistant, my job was to set up the internet business not cook. And that was a very good decision for everyone's sake.

"Good morning ladies," Dillon said, as he reached for the plate filled with bagels. Then his voice dropped from a perky tone to a more serious one. "What happened to your face?"

I thought I had covered my fresh bruise with enough makeup to disguise it. Evidently not.

"Can we discuss this up in my room?" I tilted my head toward Tilly, who had her back to us while busily rolling out pie dough.

Dillon nodded, apparently getting the point. "How was your night, Molly?"

"Slept like a baby," I said in my perky voice.

"Really," Dillon droned. "You're not just saying that to convince me of your newfound courage?"

"Nope," I replied in a light tone of voice. "Amazing, considering all the info we found last night, huh?"

Dillon seemed to realize I wasn't going to discuss this in front of Tilly. "Are you ready for a day in the basement of the Kottersville Town Hall?"

Did he just say basement?

I pulled the bagel away from my mouth. "You're kidding right? Why does everything around here have to do with basements?"

"Where do you think they keep the archives?" Dillon chortled and then took a big bite of his bagel, which had been slathered with cream cheese.

"I guess that's only logical. But how much can they have, considering this is such a small community?"

"I think you'll be surprised," Dillon said between bites. "I worked one summer helping clean out the basement and organize the record files. It was no small task."

"Well, I guess if it's that huge we'd better get going," I said. "But first, I need to show you something." I pointed up at the ceiling. "I just need you to promise to be open-minded."

Dillon's eyes widened. "Me? I'm always open-minded."

We went up the back stairs off the butler's pantry.

"Molly, I'm worried about you," Dillon said as soon as we were out of earshot from Tilly. "Did something happen last night? Something that caused that bruise on your face?"

"I'll explain it upstairs," I said and hurried ahead of him.

When we entered my room, Dillon's gaze fell on the purple dress.

I grabbed his arm before he had time to ask about it and dragged him into the bathroom. The scent of chamomile and vanilla lingered in the air. The mirror was still clear. There were no words on it.

"Last night when I was taking my bubble bath, I heard a squeaking noise," I explained. "It wasn't a door or the boards in the floor. After a couple of minutes I realized it was like a finger on a wet mirror. How did I come to that conclusion? Because there were words printed on the mirror. They spelled out '*HELP ME*.'"

With a frown, Dillon looked at the mirror. "Where are the words now? Did you wipe them off?"

"No! When the steam cleared, they were gone."

"I think I know how to bring them back, if you really didn't wipe them away," he offered.

I must have given a strange look, because he rolled his eyes at me.

"Point to where you saw the words on the mirror," he said.

I pointed to the exact spot I had seen the words the night before. He put his face close to the mirror and then exhaled onto the glass.

An "L" appeared. Then part of a "P". He exhaled several more times on the mirror. I was near to pulling him away in fear he would hyperventilate, when the words *"HELP ME"* appeared.

Dillon stepped back. His face was red and he was out of breath, but his eyes stayed riveted to the mirror.

"Unbelievable," he said. "There's got to be more to this. But how does this explain your bruise?"

"Okay, I'm coming to that," I said, happy the words were still on the mirror. "Like I said, I was taking a bubble bath and heard a squeaking noise. When I saw the words on the mirror, I jumped out of the tub. I slipped on the wet floor and fell into the vanity, catching my cheek on the way down. I ended up over there by the dumbwaiter."

"Well, that explains the bruise." He turned my face upward with one hand to check it out more closely.

"That's not the end of it," I whispered.

Startled, Dillon's hand dropped from my face. "There's more?"

"Oh, yes," I replied. "When I gained my senses after the fall, I sat on the rug wrapped in my robe and shaking like a leaf. It wasn't fear. It was from a blast of cold air." I paused a few seconds, noting the wide-eyed look on his face. "I didn't feel like I was alone. It was like the cold air accompanied something or someone that was in the room with me."

"So you think that a ghost was in this bathroom with you?" Dillon's tone turned a bit condescending, and that skeptical look returned. "You think it was the other Molly, that she printed the words on the mirror. Am I on the right track here?"

"Yes, that's precisely what I think," I answered, upset by both his tone and the look on his face. "Do you think I'm crazy?"

"No, I don't mean to doubt you." He pointed to the mirror. "I do believe you, and these words prove it."

"One more thing."

I walked out of the bathroom, pulling him with me, and then stopped dead in my tracks. I was going to show Dillon how neatly the purple dress had been arranged across my desk chair, but it wasn't there. Instead, it was now lying across my pink ruffled bed comforter.

"Okay," Dillon said. The muscles in his arms tensed, and he looked ready to strike a defensive pose. "That dress was not there when we first came in. It was lying across your desk chair. How did it get here?"

"Welcome to my world." Feeling vindicated, I swept one hand toward the dress on the bed. "Molly needs our help. She's reaching out to us in the only way she can. She has come for her dress."

"I don't think Molly has come *for* her dress," Dillon suggested. "I think she wants *you* to wear it."

"What? That's nuts. Why would she want me to wear it?"

"Humor me, please," Dillon said, raising his hands in a gesture of peace. "Just put on the dress and see what happens."

"Fine, but I don't see the point." I grabbed the dress off the bed and headed toward the bathroom.

Dillon flashed that grin I liked so much.

Stop it. Don't distract me.

I closed the bathroom door and in just a moment had donned the old dress. To my amazement, it fit perfectly.

Walking out of the bathroom, I held out the skirt and swished it around a bit. "Well?"

Smiling, Dillon grabbed my hand and pulled me inside the closet. He situated me in front of the full-length mirror, so I could see myself fully in the dress with his reflection behind me.

Then Molly's face appeared in the mirror, looking back at me as if she were wearing the dress.

With a gasp, I stumbled back into Dillon and knocked us both to the floor. When I looked up at the mirror, the other Molly was gone.

"Did you see that?" I asked, shaking like crazy.

"I did," Dillon confirmed. "It was amazing. Stand up and face the mirror again."

"Are you crazy?" I blurted, chills running through my body.

"No, listen." Dillon pulled me to my feet. "I think I get it. She wants you to wear the dress, so she can reflect in the mirror as if she's wearing it again. Don't you see? It makes sense."

That might be all well and good for him to ask, but I was the one wearing the dress and I was the one whose face was being replaced by a ghost. Then the words printed on the mirror came back to me. Maybe Dillon was right. Maybe she was reaching out to me for help.

I stepped in front of the mirror, but held my head down as if I had a new fascination for the floor. With a deep breath, I raised my head and looked in the mirror. I focused on Dillon's face over my shoulder behind me. Then I swallowed hard and stared at my face.

A young girl's face with curly blonde hair overlaid my reflection. Her eyes dropped to the dress as she examined her image. She looked back at me and our eyes locked. Her expression seemed filled with sadness. If ghosts could cry, I think she would have shed a bucketful of tears. A distinct coldness filled the closet.

I felt an icy touch on my hand and jerked back. Goosebumps rose on my arms, causing the hair to stand straight up.

"What's wrong?" Dillon asked.

"I think she just touched my hand," I said.

"Can you get her to do it again?" Dillon asked. "I think you may have set up a form of communication with Molly."

I didn't know much about ghosts. They hadn't exactly offered Ghosts 101 at my last high school.

Slowly, I stretched my hand toward the mirror. I felt the icy touch again, but this time I saw her hand reflect on mine. He was right. She was trying to make a connection with me.

"Talk to her," Dillon said, excited. "Ask her a question."

"What do you want me to say? How's your day going?"

"Ask her what she wants," Dillon suggested. "Was she the one who wrote the words on the mirror? Why does she need our help?"

I considered my options. Now that she had finally made contact, I didn't want to frighten her away. That was a funny thought. I was worried about frightening away a ghost. I decided to start simple.

"Are you Molly Greyson?" I asked in as calm a voice as possible.

The ghost nodded her head up and down.

I swallowed trying to contain my surprise as I realized we were actually communicating.

"Do you know who I am?" I asked.

The ghost once again nodded.

This time I took a long low breath.

Dillon stood behind me with a look of disbelief. "Unbelievable," he whispered.

I gathered my courage. "Did you write the words on my mirror?"

The ghost nodded again, but this time she looked frightened.

"Are you afraid of something, someone?" I asked quickly.

"Yes—*help me*," she answered in a wavering voice. "*Please find proof.*"

She stopped and turned her head, as if to look behind her. "*He's coming.*"

I jerked back, pulling my hand from her grasp. When she turned back around her face was filled with terror. She reached out with both hands and grabbed my hand again.

A cold wind blew through the closet strong enough to rip clothes off their hangers. The force of the gale pushed me back into Dillon. I felt her grasp snapped away, as though she was being pulled by a great force.

Just as quickly as the wind came, it was gone and so was Molly. I looked back into the mirror and saw only my own reflection.

"What was that?" Dillon asked. His hair was pushed back, as if he had been riding a motorcycle without a helmet.

"I think—" I paused to consider my words. "I think that was the 'thing' Molly is afraid of. It's why she needs our help."

"She asked us to find proof," Dillon said. "Find proof of what?"

"Something the other being doesn't want anyone to know," I replied. "Why else would it take her away so suddenly?"

I went to the bathroom and changed out of the purple dress. Would I see Molly again? If not, how would we help her if we didn't know what she needed protection from?

It took me only a minute to don my regular clothing. Then I emerged from the bathroom.

"I think we're on the right path," I said with determination. "Molly wants us to find proof of something. We just don't know what we're looking for. The only way we're going to help her is to do what we already have planned. We need to get down to the Town Hall and search through those records."

"Let's get going," Dillon said. "I have a feeling this other being won't be pleased, once it finds out we're helping her."

I agreed. Whatever had snatched Molly out of the mirror was obviously not happy with her communicating with us. We had stirred up another being, possibly another ghost. Whatever it was, it had the power to affect the natural world and that made it dangerous.

The sooner we found what Molly needed from us, the safer it would be for everyone.

CHAPTER 19

THE drive to the Town Hall was a quiet one.

Dillon seemed deep in thought, and my brain was working overtime to make sense of everything that had happened.

Who would have thought two weeks ago that I would be assisting a ghost with some unresolved business? I looked down at my hand. Dillon was steering with one hand while holding my hand with his other one. A warm feeling swept over me. At least I had Dillon to help me.

When we arrived at the receptionist desk, we were greeted by an elderly lady with silvery hair that seemed to glisten even in the harsh florescent lighting. Her cheeks were rosy with an over-abundance of blush. Her wrinkly hands were accented by manicured red fingernails.

"My word, if it isn't the young Darby boy." The elderly lady pulled a slight smile. "How's your Mama doing these days running that Bed and Breakfast? She'll be having her hands full with fall coming on and the tourists coming to see the foliage." Then she looked at me. "Oh, I'm sorry. I'm rambling. Don't get too many visitors. How may I be of assistance to you and your lovely lady friend?"

"Hello, Mrs. Hill," Dillon said. "You're looking very stylish today."

His compliment turned Mrs. Hill's cheeks a deeper scarlet.

"This is Molly Greyson," he said in a rather formal introduction. "She and her family are the new residents of the Kotter estate. We're here to do some research in the records room. Would it be possible to get in today?"

The little old lady's face lost its rosiness, when Dillon mentioned the Kotter estate. "Now why would two young people with so much to do want to spend their time down in a dark basement going through dusty old records?"

"Molly has some questions and I thought I could help her," Dillon explained.

Mrs. Hill just stood, as if she had no intention of letting anyone into that basement to see the archives.

"It's for a school project. History class, I think. Right Molly?" He looked at me, eyes pleading for some assistance.

"Um, yes," I added. "It's for History class. Since I'm new here, I want to impress my teachers."

"Very well," Mrs. Hill droned with a suspicious look in her eyes.

She reached into the drawer beneath the desk and retrieved a key. She rose out of her chair very slowly and hobbled toward the door that read: *No Public Admittance – Employees only.* She turned the key with some difficulty given the condition of her arthritic hands, and then pushed open the door.

Dillon and I practically rushed through the opening.

"Thanks so much, Mrs. Hill," Dillon said, pulling the door shut behind us.

"Wait!" Mrs. Hill called through the door. "I didn't think school started for a few more days yet."

Too late. We were already inside. There was no turning back.

The stairs were dark and narrow. Just like every other building in downtown Kottersville, this one was old. Whatever renovations had been made to it must have been limited to the upper rooms, neglecting the basement. Fortunately there was a tile floor, but it still smelled musty and dust filled the air.

"How can anything survive the years in this damp place?" I asked.

"Oh, don't worry," Dillon said. "The records we're looking for aren't here. Remember, I told you I worked here one summer reorganizing the records. Follow me."

We walked down a cramped hallway lit with row after row of those annoying long florescent bulbs. We passed two doors that were recessed from the hall about two feet. I hoped Dillon knew where he was going.

Then I saw a door at the end of the long hall. Dillon stopped and pressed a code into an electronic keypad. The pad lights changed from red to green. It was definitely more modern than I had expected.

"What?" Dillon gave a casual shrug. "I figured they hadn't changed the code, since no one is allowed in here without a guard. Mrs. Hill thinks we're just going to go through the records in the main room. She won't expect me to know the security code."

Dillon entered first, and I followed close behind.

Out of the corner of my eye, I could have sworn I saw something duck into the recessed area of the first door we passed. It must have been my big imagination at work from too much ghost hunting.

To my surprise behind the keypad locked door there was a very clean and neatly organized room. Those awful overhead florescent lights had been replaced by pleasant table lamps. As I walked around, I realized this wasn't just a room. It was a small underground warehouse. Rows of filing cabinets covered both sides of the room. At the end of the filing cabinets sat large plastic boxes. Some were labeled with names and others with numbers.

I pulled out one of the lower boxes and opened it. Inside were books, jewelry boxes, and china dishes. It was what some people might call artifacts. I saw them as pieces from a person's life, someone who had passed on with no heirs. I opened one jewelry box and saw a strand of pearls and a gold sleeve bracelet. They looked very old and expensive. No wonder this place was sealed behind a secure keypad. I looked at the name on the end of the container. Nattress. Not a name I knew, but then I was the new kid on the block.

"Do you think there might be boxes with the Kotter name on them?" I asked Dillon, as I began searching through the lower boxes. "Maybe there's one with Greyson."

"I thought we came down here to research the written records not go through people's belongings," Dillon chided. "We need to focus on why we're here. To find something that gives us a reason to understand why Molly is so scared."

Dillon was right. I needed to focus. But I knew once this was settled I'd be back searching for a box with the Greyson name on it.

We went to the cabinet with the letters GRA-GRO on the front. Dillon flipped through the file folders until he came to GREYSON. I noticed the file was larger than most of the others next to it. He carried it over and placed it on one of the large oak tables. We both sat down in the high-backed rolling desk chairs and stared at the file.

"I think you should do the honors, since it has your name on it," Dillon said respectfully.

Anxious yet afraid of what I might find, I flipped open the cover. There were a lot of words in nearly illegible handwriting.

"How are we going to ever make sense of this?" I asked.

"Most of these files were written decades ago," Dillon said. "A lot of the writing will be faded or hard to make out. The oldest files will probably be toward the back. Keep going. There should be dates in the top right hand corner, if I remember correctly." He reached across the table and pulled a magnifying glass from a pencil container. "Use this."

I took the magnifying glass and found it did make deciphering the faded text much easier in some places. I found dates where he said and with some straining I was able to read them. There were a lot of names and dates. Some had addresses and cities listed, as well. There were birth and death records and even marriage certificates neatly arranged by decade. I had no idea how old Molly was when she had died. Her ghostly reflection looked about my age, but I didn't have a clue in what year she might have been born. But I did know that one photo was dated 1886, so it had to be before that.

"I guess the only way to find Molly is to start searching birth records and work our way from the back to the front of this file," I suggested.

It was going to be a long day going this route, but it seemed the only logical approach. Dillon agreed.

I flipped to the very back of the file packet and magnified the date in the corner of the page: *May 1831*. Wow! That was a long time ago.

"What's the date on the city limit sign?" I asked.

"You mean when the town was founded by Benjamin Kotter? That was 1886."

"Hmmm." I looked through the magnifier again just to be sure. "This file is dated long before that. Why would files be kept before a town is established? Wouldn't it be reasonable to assume records would start with the founding of the town?"

"I think before the town was established, there were just territories," Dillon explained. "Towns were named after the person or persons who set up the first buildings. After several buildings were established, then it would become an official town. I learned that in Indiana History class my Freshman year."

Well, that was most impressive. Dillon was much smarter than any jock I had met in California.

I scanned down the short list of names. There were a few different surnames listed other than Greyson, presumably from marriages since there were no marriage certificates in the files back this far. Most of the men had farmer or carpenter listed as their occupation and the women were listed as homemaker or teacher.

I was already into the 1840's when I came across a name I recognized: William Greyson. That was my father's name. The date of birth was 1840, but what caught my attention beyond the name was his occupation. It was listed as architect/contractor. He was the first one I had noticed that could possibly have gone to college and earned a degree. I pulled out his records and placed them closer to the lamp. His wife's name was Laura. This was getting creepier by the minute. My mom's name was Lara. I scanned down the list to the place where children were listed. And there it was, a girl named Molly with a birth date of 1870.

With a quick bit of mental math, I figured out that Molly had been sixteen when the 1886 photo had been taken. I scanned to the bottom column where the date of death was listed. There were no dates of death for any of them, only the word *'Unknown'*.

Sitting back in the chair, I placed my fingertips to my temples.

"What's wrong?" Dillon asked. "Too many numbers and names for your brain to process?"

I sat for a few moments, trying to make sense of the information. Finally, I looked over at Dillon. "I think I have found our Molly."

"That's great! So that means we can stop here and move onto the Kotter files. Let me see what you found."

Dillon reached for the file in front of me, but I jerked it away.

"Why'd you do that?" he asked. "Is there something you don't want me to see?"

I knew I owed Dillon an explanation. "This file is totally not what I expected. I'm having a hard time making sense of this."

"Well, I told you some of the files would be hard to read," Dillon said and held out one hand. "Here. Let me see if I can help."

"Okay." I pushed the file in front of him and opened the cover. "Let me walk you through this."

"I think I can read it on my own, thank you," Dillon grumbled.

"I didn't mean it to sound that way," I apologized. "Hold on to your seat because this is very close to unbelievable. I found this file with William Greyson. That's my dad's name. His wife's name was listed as Laura with a U. My mom's name is Lara without the U. Their only child was Molly. Are you seeing where this is going? My name and her name are both the same, Molly."

"Holy cow! How can this be so—so identical to your family?" Dillon sounded as stunned as he looked. "Did you find Molly's birth date?"

"Yes," I said. "It's listed as 1870. That would make her sixteen when the photo dated 1886 was taken. That's the same age as I am now."

"What about the date of death?" Dillon asked.

"Well, this is where it begins to get even weirder. Every other file I read through listed dates of death. When I scanned down to that column in this file it was listed as *'Unknown'*."

"Unknown?"

"Not only for Molly," I whispered. "For Laura and William, as well."

"What? No. That's got to be an error. How can there not be a date of death for all three? They just didn't fall off the face of the earth. Maybe they moved and died somewhere else." Dillon turned to the second page and scanned the information on it. "Did you see this? Their last known address is 2136 Lafayette Road. Sound familiar?"

I nearly choked when Dillon read the address. The Kotter estate was at 2136 Lafayette Road. It was my address.

"Molly wasn't just a visitor or guest at a party," I said. "That photo wasn't of the Kotter family. It was of the Greyson family. Molly actually lived in my house."

CHAPTER 20

DILLON jumped up and nearly ran to the filing cabinet marked KAR-KUT. I followed, trying to keep up.

Wildly, he flipped through the files. Then he stopped at one marked KOTTER. He rushed back to the desk and tossed the file onto it. After pulling open the cover, he began to read. His finger moved down the page, his eyes following every name. He flipped to the next page and his finger hovered for a moment over one name: Benjamin Kotter.

I read along as his fingers continued to scan the columns. Kotter's birth date was listed as 1821. He was married to Penelope Crawford Kotter. They had two children, Benjamin II and Geraldine. At the bottom of the column was his date of death: 1907. I grabbed a piece of paper and did the calculations. He had died at age 86. Penelope died in 1906. Then, oddly enough, the now familiar word *'Unknown'* was listed in the date of death column under his children.

Disbelief, surprise, and a million questions flew through my brain.

I looked at Dillon. His face said everything I was feeling right now.

He flipped to the next page. I didn't wait on his fingers to lead me down the page this time. My eyes dropped immediately to the column marked *'Last Known Address'*.

"Enough is enough," I said out loud. The address listed was 2136 Lafayette Road. My house. "If I understand this correctly, my ancestors lived in this house from the time it was built until 1886. Then from 1886 to his death, Benjamin Kotter lived there with *his* family." I paused to organize my thoughts. My brain was in overdrive. "Who really built the house? John the realtor said Benjamin Kotter built the house and lived there the rest of his life. Everyone in Kottersville believes that. But how can that be true if the records say the Greyson's lived there first? Did William Greyson really build the house and then in 1886 sold it to Benjamin Kotter? If so, where did the Greyson's go?"

"I might be able to track down some information in another area that would answer a lot," Dillon said.

His chair squeaked as he got to his feet. He headed toward a door on the left side of the room. There he punched in numbers on another keypad, but it did not flash to green.

"Rats," Dillon grumbled.

He tried another code, but the light remained red and the door did not open.

"Have you forgotten the code or have they changed it?" I asked impatiently.

"Let me concentrate," Dillon muttered. "There were three codes for this door."

He closed his eyes, and I stood next to him as quiet as a mouse. In a moment his eyes popped open and he punched more numbers into the keypad. This time the light went from red to green. The handle gave a loud click and the sound of tumblers turning echoed. A special room with that much security surely held the best kept secrets.

After opening the door, Dillon stepped into the room and switched on a light.

The side room was much smaller. It was filled with filing cabinets made of wood with brass handles. We walked down the first row of cabinets, examining the information cards on the front of each drawer. There were no names on the cards, just dates.

"What's inside these cabinets, more personal files?" I asked.

"No, not personal files," Dillon explained. "These drawers hold the deeds in Kottersville. The ones on the other side of the room have microfilm of old newspaper articles. Some even have entire newspapers on microfilm."

"What are you looking for exactly? Maybe I can help. Two sets of eyes are better than one."

"I'm looking for the drawer dated 1880-1890 for the house deeds. The deed to the Kotter Estate should be in there. Got it!" He opened a drawer and searched through folders. "That's strange. The file for 1886 is missing."

"I don't think it's strange at all. I think someone doesn't want us to find the folder." I remembered the movement I saw in the hallway right before we stepped into the records room. "Let me look."

I removed all the folders from that drawer, hoping the file was just out of order. Nothing. I started to place the folders back in the drawer, when a wooden panel fell forward revealing a secret compartment. Inside was a folder marked 1886.

Bingo!

I raised my eyebrows at Dillon, positive this was what we were looking for.

I saw that there were smaller tables in the deeds room. There was also a microfilm reader in one corner. We sat close together and opened the folder. There were only about ten certificates of ownership in it.

"Here it is," Dillon said. "It says William Greyson signed over legal rights to Benjamin Kotter on April 27, 1886, for an undisclosed sum. That answers one question. Benjamin Kotter didn't build the estate. The Greyson's lived there first. Why is it listed as an undisclosed sum?"

"Let's look for files that date back a few more years to see if we can determine when William Greyson bought the house and from whom." Then something dawned on me. "His occupation was listed as an architect. Could he have been the builder?"

"Good question. Let's find out." Dillon returned to the cabinets in search of proof. He brought ten years of folders and plopped them in front of me. Then he divided them up between us. "Two sets of eyes, you said."

I flipped the first folder open and scanned the top of the first certificate, looking for familiar names. After going through three folders from different years, I found one with William Greyson's name at the top. It was dated February 27, 1876, but the rest of the writing had been smeared beyond recognition. The ink ran down in dried blue rivers, covering the rest of the certificate. The paper was wrinkled, as if something had been spilled on it. "Now what?"

"Now we go to the microfilms," Dillon said. "Maybe, just maybe, the auditors made a copy of the deed before it was damaged and recorded it on microfilm."

When we reached the cabinet with the microfilm, we saw it was locked with a padlock.

"Great," I grumbled. "Any suggestions?"

Dillon put his hand on my head and began pulling at my bun.

"Hey!" I squawked, trying to pull away from his tugging hands. "What are you doing? Have you gone mad?"

"How do you hold that thing in place? Do you have any pins in it?"

I reached up, pulled out a hairpin, and handed it to him. "Will this do, MacGyver?"

"Perfect," Dillon said.

After straightening the pin, he dug carefully at the padlock keyhole. In the dead silence of the underground bunker, I heard a faint click and then another click. Finally, the padlock fell open.

"Wallah!" he announced with a grin.

Again Dillon searched through what looked like tiny old digital camera cards. He held up one to the light. With a nod, he walked over to the microfilm reader and turned it on with the push of a button. Then he placed the small card into the machine. A light came on, enlarging what was on the film.

Suddenly, there was a loud pounding on the door, which sent both of us jumping out of our chairs.

"You aren't supposed to be in there!" a man screamed through the locked door. "That's a restricted area!"

"Hurry," I said. "Find the certificate we need before we get in big trouble."

"I'm trying," Dillon replied, his head bent over the lighted display screen. "I'm in 1878. So far nothing, wait, here it is. It's listed under the year 1876. Listen to this. *New deed and title issued on February, 27, 1876, to William Greyson, builder and owner of Greyson Manor. Newly assigned address: 2136 Lafayette Road, Greysontown, Indiana.*"

I felt my mouth drop open.

"It was Greysontown *before* it was Kottersville?" Dillon seemed as surprised as I was. "This gets more interesting by the minute."

The man pounded louder this time. Dillon pulled out his phone and took a picture of the screen on the microfilm reader. Then he pulled the microfilm card out of the reader slot, just as the door swung open to reveal the angry face of a security guard.

I saw Dillon drop the card into the front pocket of his jeans.

Behind my back I was holding the Kotter deed. As carefully and quietly as possible, I folded the paper it into a tiny square and hid it in my hand.

"Just what do you think you kids are doing in this room?" the guard demanded. "And how did you get in here in the first place? This is a secure room. No admittance to the public."

The guard pushed Dillon and me ahead of him and out of the room.

I managed to slip the small square of paper inside my blouse. Dillon saw what I had done and seemed to be fighting not to smile.

"We were just doing some research for Molly's History class," Dillon said in his most innocent hometown boy voice. "We explained to Mrs. Hill why we needed to come down here. She unlocked the door for us."

The guard grumbled something unintelligible. "Get out of here. And the next time you need to do research in the basement, you'll need an adult with you. Understand?"

"Yes, sir," Dillon said in a respectful tone and even managed to look properly contrite. "Sorry, sir. It won't happen again."

Mrs. Hill stood by her desk with her arms crossed and one foot tapping in a huff.

As we passed by her, I offered my meekest smile while Dillon continued to look innocent.

The guard shoved us out the front door and slammed it shut behind us. Then he flipped the OPEN sign to CLOSED.

Dillon and I walked calmly but quickly to his car.

Once inside the car, we laughed until we were both wheezing.

Looking quite pleased with himself, Dillon pulled the microfilm card from his jeans.

I reached into my blouse and pulled out the folded deed. "Now all we have to do is figure out how this helps Molly."

CHAPTER 21

AS we drove up the long driveway to the estate, I noticed an unfamiliar car parked out front.

"Looks like we have company," I said. Then my heart raced and I began to shake. "Do you think we're in trouble already?"

"Calm down," Dillon said. "There's no way the Town Manager could have beaten us here. No one in this town ever moves that fast."

At least there were no police decals on the car. That was good news.

Dillon drove his car around to the back by the carriage house garage, and we entered through the glorified mud room.

I stopped dead in my tracks, when I saw who was sitting at the bar across from Mom.

Dylan from California was having a conversation with my mom in my kitchen.

"What are *you* doing here?" I asked, almost shouting.

"Well, it's good to see you, too, Molly," California Dylan responded, looking less than pleased.

"That's no way to treat a friend who has come over two thousand miles to see you," Mom scolded.

Indiana Dillon, gentleman that he was, offered a hand to California Dylan. "Hi. I'm Dillon. Nice to meet you."

"I can see that Molly isn't going to do introductions, so I'll introduce myself," Dylan said with force. "I'm also Dylan. From California. Molly's boyfriend."

Dillon pulled back his hand and looked at me.

I was mortified. How could Dylan just show up unannounced from California, knowing he was unwelcome here? The nerve of him! He was brash and egotistical. How could I have missed that in the past? How stupid I had been. But no more.

"Well, aren't you going to say anything, Molly?" Dylan said.

I looked at Dillon to rescue me from this bad dream.

"I think you two have a few things to sort out, so I'm going to head out," Dillon said. Then he tossed me stern look. "We can talk later."

I pleaded with my eyes for Dillon not to leave, but he turned and walked toward the door.

"Stop!" I called. "This won't take long. Would you please just wait on the porch bench?"

Dillon turned and gave a quick nod. I knew he didn't want to leave me alone with some California playboy any more than I wanted him to.

"Why don't you show Dylan around the estate?" Mom suggested. "It will give you some privacy, some time to talk and get reacquainted."

Great. Was she on California Dylan's side now? What load of lies had he been feeding her?

With reluctance, I led Dylan out the back door through the mud room, far away from Dillon on the front porch. I headed across the pasture and did not stop until we stood under the weeping willow tree.

"Listen, Dylan," I started, surprised by the firmness in my voice, "we need to get something straight. First of all, I'm not your girlfriend anymore. This long distance thing won't work. Besides, from the phone conversation we had two weeks ago, it was clear that you had a new girlfriend. Robyn confirmed it. And second, I have a new boyfriend."

"You mean that blue collar hayseed? You've got to be joking." Dylan moved closer to me. "How can you resist what I have to offer?"

He leaned in to kiss me, but I slapped him hard across the face.

"Oww!" he complained. "What's gotten into you? You never resisted my kisses before. As a matter of fact, you asked for them."

I reared back and this time curled my hand into a tight fist. With power I didn't know was inside me, I landed a blow squarely on his jaw.

Dylan backed off rubbing his face. He wiped his mouth with his hand and saw a few drops of blood. "Girl, you've changed. I'm not certain I like the change."

"Well, it's not up to you to decide. I like the new me. Sorry if I disappoint you." I felt pride. I rubbed my aching hand behind my back, but the pain was well worth it.

"So you have a new beau," he said in a condescending tone. "I bet you haven't made any more new friends. You always depended on me to let you join my circle of friends. You never were Miss Popularity."

"You'd be surprised at my new friends."

"I don't see any beating down your door," he pushed.

A wicked thought popped into my head.

"That's because they're already up in my room waiting for me," I said in a coy voice.

"Yeah, your Mom told me about your round room," Dylan said as he backed me into the tree. I could already see the wheels turning in his head. "How about taking me to see it? I'm sure *your friends* will give us some private time to reconcile our differences."

He had his agenda. I had mine.

"Okay, let's go," I said.

When we entered the kitchen, Mom was fighting to roll out an uncooperative ball of pie dough.

"Mom, can you show Dylan around the house while I straighten up my room?" I asked. "Give me about ten minutes, please."

After all, what could Dylan do in front of my Mom? He was always pleasant and courteous to parents. Sure enough, he gave Mom his best and most gracious fake smile.

Yep, two-faced jerk.

I raced to the front door and quickly spilled my plan to Dillon. He looked pleased.

"Are you sure you don't need help?" he asked in a quiet voice.

"No," I said with confidence. "Wait here. This won't take long."

I bounded up the steps, hoping to allow enough time to set my plan in motion before Dylan walked into my room. I flung open the closet door and stood in front of the mirror.

"Molly?" I whispered.

Immediately, Molly's figure appeared in the reflection.

"I need your help," I said. Then I filled her in on the plan.

She nodded. I could see real joy in her face. Joy she might not have felt in a long, long time.

I shut the closet door and sat on my bed, waiting for Mom and Dylan to arrive.

It wasn't long before there was a soft knock on the door.

"Molly, is the room decent?" Mom asked.

"Yep, come on in," I replied.

Mom and Dylan walked into an organized, clean room. I could tell by the grin on her face that Mom was pleased with my new housekeeping abilities.

"Well, I'll go back to wrestling with that pie dough," Mom said. "If you need anything I'll be in the kitchen." She backed out of the room and shut the door behind her.

Dylan walked around the room and did not appear to miss any details. "Pink ruffles and a canopy bed. Really? Boy, have you changed. Although I have to admit this room is pretty awesome. Your mom told me you have the third floor to yourself. Where exactly are all the friends you said were waiting for you in here? I bet if you screamed, no one would hear you way up here."

He walked close to my bed and put his hand on my knee.

I jumped up and headed toward the closet. "Want to see how enormous my closet is? It's practically as big as my old bedroom."

Dylan slammed me into the door and tried to press his mouth on mine.

Something from inside the closet pushed the door with such great force that Dylan and I went tumbling to the floor. I knew it had been Molly. She was waiting for us.

"Sorry, I guess I got a little over anxious," I lied.

Dylan got up and headed for me again only this time he had an angry look on his face.

I quickly pushed open the closet door and lead him inside. "See, isn't it great?"

I walked over to the mirror. Dylan walked up and stood very close to me. Too close.

Molly's reflection appeared.

Dylan was concentrating so hard on wrapping his arms around my waist and burying his face in my hair, that at first he didn't look up in the mirror. Then he jerked and backed up a couple of steps.

"What was that?" he squeaked. "Your hands are like ice."

I stepped to the side, so he would be standing directly in front of the mirror.

Sure enough, Molly's full figure reflected in the mirror back at him.

A confused expression washed across his face.

"Dylan," I said, gesturing toward the mirror. "Meet my good friend, Molly."

"Is this some kind of lame joke? Are you going off the deep end out here in Nowheresville?"

"*I am not a joke,*" Molly said in that whispery, watery voice. "*I am Molly's friend. And you need to leave.*"

Without warning, she stepped out of the mirror and stood directly in front of Dylan. She was nearly transparent, standing before us in her long gown. Her breath filled the air with an icy coldness. The closet door slammed shut behind us with a loud thud. She floated in a continuous circle around Dylan, wrapping him in a cloud of chilly vapor. He began to shake violently.

"Stop!" Dylan screamed. "Make it stop! This is insane!"

"Remember, we are on the third floor," I reminded him. "Most likely no one can hear your screams way up here."

I watched as Molly kept him encased in her spidery web of frost, unable to move. I had no idea she could actually appear outside of the mirror.

"Are you ready to leave me alone and promise to never come back to Indiana again?" I asked, as calmly as possible.

"Yes, yes, anything," Dylan begged, shivering. "I promise never to speak your name again if you just get this thing away from me. Please, Molly, help me!"

I nodded to Molly and the icy hold she had over Dylan evaporated. She floated back into the mirror, gave a quick wink over her shoulder, and was gone.

Dylan crumbled to the floor. On his hands and knees, he crawled to the door and grabbed the handle trying to stand. He was weak, shaken, and barely able to speak. His golden tan skin had taken on an ashen hue and ice crystals fell from his blonde hair. A strange streak of white hair ran across the right side of his head.

"Please," he pleaded. "Let me out of here."

I felt Molly had accomplished exactly what we had set out to do. I didn't need to rub it in or rehash the event. Although it would be sweet revenge if I could tell his friends how frightened he was in my closet. No, I decided to take the adult approach and leave it alone. He was on his way out and that's all I wanted to accomplish. I wasn't worried that he would tell anyone about the ghost in my closet. But once he was home he would probably contrive some elaborate story for his friends that I begged him to stay. Then he would put his spin on it and say he made the trip to end it with me and he was being kind to me by doing it in person. Blah, blah, blah. I knew him well enough to know he would never let anyone know how scared he was.

I followed Dylan out of my bedroom. Still shaking, he managed to get down the steep stairs from the third floor. His hair was dripping from the melting ice crystals. By the time he reached the kitchen he was shaking from a cold sweat.

"Are you leaving so soon?" Mom asked.

Dylan didn't stop to answer. He just kept heading toward the back door.

"Well, then," Mom said, looking unruffled. "Have a safe flight back to California."

Dylan stumbled out of the kitchen, through the mud room, and right into Dillon waiting on the back porch.

"In a hurry?" Dillon asked with that gorgeous grin.

Without a single remark, Dylan staggered around Dillon. He piled into the rental car, slammed the door, and cranked the engine to life. With tires spinning, he drove through the flower bed and then pulled the car back onto the driveway.

"You people are a bunch of deranged freaks!" he yelled out the window.

Then the car fishtailed wildly down the curving driveway.

Dillon and I did a high five, and then laughed.

"Come here you little freak," Dillon said.

He pulled me to him and kissed me. It was a very good kiss.

After a moment, we went back into the kitchen, where Mom was pulling a frozen pie shell out of the freezer.

"Whoops," she said, startled. "Caught me. Don't tell Dad. I fought with the other dough until it finally won. Was Dylan okay? He must have taken it really hard when you told him you two were over. His face was so white he looked like he had seen a ghost."

CHAPTER 22

AFTER racing Dillon up the stairs, I fell backwards on my bed.

Dillon sat on the bed beside me. "Girl, that was totally awesome. From the look on Dylan's face, I'd say he did see a ghost. So fill me in. What did Molly do to him?"

"You are not going to believe this," I said, sitting up next to Dillon. "Molly came out of the mirror and into the closet with us. What she did to him made me very glad she's on our side."

"Do you think she'll come out again if we go in and call for her?" Dillon asked.

"I don't know. We can try."

I headed toward the closet. A few drops of moisture remained on the wooden floor. I stepped in front of the mirror and spoke Molly's name. She didn't appear as she did earlier. I called her name again.

Suddenly, an unfamiliar face appeared in the mirror. It felt as if pure evil was staring at me.

I stumbled, pushing Dillon backward with me.

That gave the entity just enough room to step out of the mirror and into the closet.

He was an old man of about eighty years or more, bald on top with long grey hair on the sides. His wrinkled face was drawn into a frown with furrows between his eyebrows. He hovered a few inches above the floor and stared at us with dark eyes.

The air turned so cold, that I could see my breath coming out in puffs. Then the closet door slammed behind us, trapping me and Dillon in there with an angry spirit.

"Who do you think you are contacting souls from my existence?" the ghost asked in a deep, crackling voice that sounded like it was being played through the speaker horn of an antique phonograph. *"Leave Molly alone. Leave us both alone. Vacate this house. It is not yours to take!"*

"And just who are you to be handing out orders?" Dillon asked the ghost.

I was shaking in my boots, but Dillon sounded ready to fight.

A deafening rumble of laughter reverberated through the closet.

"Who am I?" The ghost gave another deep, evil laugh. *"I am Benjamin Kotter, owner of this house."*

This was Benjamin Kotter's ghost? I had not found one single photo of him in the stack from the basement. Nor was he in any of the framed photos on the walls of the ballroom. That struck me as odd.

"You're not the owner anymore," Dillon stated without a hint of trepidation. "The Greyson's now own this house. It was built by William Greyson, and now it has returned to the original family."

"And where did you come up with such blasphemy?" The ghost seemed to quiver in anger. *"The Greyson's do not deserve to own such a grand house. Heed my warning, boy. Your lives will be in danger if they choose to stay."*

Kotter rose into the air and swirled around us at such a great speed that ice crystals formed on our hair and clothing.

Dillon pulled me around and reached for the door knob. His fingers slipped on the now icy brass knob. After a couple of tries, he got the knob to turn. He pulled open the door and dragged me out of the closet. Using his free hand, he slammed the door shut behind us. Then he shoved my desk chair under the knob to hold the door in place.

Dillon sat me on the bed and then proceeded to wrap me up in my comforter, every blanket in sight, and ever a small shag rug from the floor. All he left was a small opening for my nose and eyes.

As he stood over me, ice began to melt from his hair. Water dripped down his face.

Loud crashing noises erupted from my closet, and the door knob rattled. Kotter was in a rage, throwing a ghostly tantrum. But why wasn't he coming out after us to finish the ice storm had he started?

I tried to get out of my blanket cocoon, but Dillon held the folds with an iron grip.

"Stay still until you warm up," he said through chattering teeth.

I managed to pull the blanket away from my mouth. "You're freezing, too."

With a shrug, Dillon unwrapped the cocoon just enough to pull him inside with me. We sat there on the bed, shivering together and staring at the closet door.

Then everything fell silent.

"Do you think he'll come after us?" I asked in a whisper, terrified of the answer.

"For some reason, these ghosts don't seem to be able to pass through doors or walls," Dillon said. "All the movies I've ever seen show ghosts going through walls. Either the movies got it wrong, or these ghosts are different somehow."

"It seems to me their only way out is through that mirror," I said.

"My exact thoughts," Dillon agreed.

We sat for a long time together, until our shivers turned into sweat and we dropped the weight of the blankets around us.

"It seems pretty calm in there," Dillon said, getting to his feet. "I think I'll check it out."

"Stop!" I sputtered, pulling on the back of his shirt. "Don't go in there. He might still be waiting to attack."

"We have to go back in there sometime," Dillon replied. "I might as well be first."

He pulled out of my grasp and walked toward the closet door.

I launched off the bed and followed close behind him. As I passed my desk, I grabbed my old cheerleader baton and held it in the air like a weapon.

Dillon looked back at the baton and raised one eyebrow. "Do you really think that will protect us against a ghost?"

Feeling silly, I dropped the baton and stayed a few inches behind him.

As quietly as possible, he pulled the chair away from the door knob. Then he turned the knob and pushed open the door. Cold air rushed out, causing me to blink back tears. The ghost was gone, but my closet was a total disaster with clothes and shoes tossed everywhere.

I grabbed my bathrobe and tossed it over the mirror to cover our reflections.

"Maybe that will keep him in while I clean up my closet," I said, disgusted at the mess he had left in his wake.

We spent the next half hour hanging up clothes and placing shoes back in their boxes.

Then I heard a soft voice.

"Shhhh," I whispered to Dillon.

We stood still and listened.

"It's Molly," the voice said more loudly this time.

I yanked the robe from the mirror and saw Molly's face.

"I only have a few minutes," Molly said in her ethereal voice. *"I saw what Benjamin did to you. I am so sorry. As long as you remain in this house, you are not safe. This is the only portal I know. You must break the mirror."*

"Molly, I'm so glad you're alright. I was afraid Kotter had attacked you, too." I stared into her sad eyes. "But if I break the mirror, you won't have a portal anymore, either. Isn't there another way we can rid this house of him and still keep in contact with you? Maybe an exorcist could help."

"If they came and blessed the house, it would remove us both. I have just met you. I want to stay and be your friend." A new expression crossed Molly's face. *"There is one other way, but I worry that it will be too dangerous for you."*

"Tell us before he returns," Dillon urged.

I nodded in agreement.

Molly looked back over her shoulder in panic. *"The only other way is to lure him outside. If he leaves the house, he will never be able to return."*

Before we could ask any more questions Molly was gone.

I turned to Dillon who looked as stunned as I felt.

"How do we do that?" I asked. "How do we get him outside before he can harm us first?"

"Let me think for a minute." Dillon pursed his lips and tapped one foot. "We know we don't want to break the mirror. Molly might be left alone with Kotter forever. So we do exactly what she said. We lure him out of the mirror." Dillon stepped into the doorway. "Out of the closet." He looked across my bedroom. "Then out the window."

I stood beside Dillon in the closet doorway. I looked back at the now covered mirror and then glanced out at the bedroom windows. "Just how do you propose luring this ghost outside, when I'm pretty sure he knows that's not a good place for him to be?"

There was a knock on the door. We both jumped.

"Molly, everything okay up here?" Mom asked. She opened the bedroom door and leaned through the opening. "What was all that crashing?"

"Everything's okay in here," I replied.

Then I saw Mom eyeing our wet clothes and the pile of blankets on the floor.

"Sorry for the mess," I said and tried to appear innocent. "We were having a water balloon fight. We'll clean it up."

Mom looked at the mess and then at us. "Isn't that a little juvenile? Really, water balloons in the house? I'll be back later to make sure this mess is cleaned up." She gave me one more suspicious look and then left, shutting the door behind her.

"Quick thinking," Dillon said, patting me on the head like a child. "A bit lame, but it looks like she bought it."

"For now," I muttered and then looked up at him. "Any ideas on how to trick a vicious ghost into leaving this house?"

Dillon studied the one long window in the bedroom. Then he headed out the door toward the ballroom. I couldn't imagine what was going on in his brain, but I followed closely behind. He walked right up to the old tapestry, the one that covered the elevator shaft.

"I think this will do nicely," Dillon announced.

"Oh," I said, nodding. "I see where you're going with this."

* * *

DILLON lifted the heavy tapestry off the floor. It took both of us to carry it to my bedroom.

He sent me in search of nails and a hammer, which I found on a shelf in the mud room. When I returned with tools in hand, he had pushed my desk to one side.

After a couple of tugs, he managed to open the old window all the way. Fortunately, the screens had not yet been added.

With a groan, he lifted the tapestry in place. At the top right, he hammered in one nail just enough to hold without being too secure. Then he did the same with a second nail on the top left.

"Okay, that's done," I said, admiring his work. "Now how do we—"

Dillon put his finger to my lips.

"I saw a wagon filled with hay out by the barn," he explained in a low voice. "I used to do what we call 'barn diving' when I was a kid. You put a tractor full of hay under the top barn window. Then dive in, pretending it's a pool of water." He flashed a mischievous grin. "I had the front layout mastered by the time I was eleven."

"We're on the third floor," I reminded, looking at the tapestry and then back at him. "I don't know if I can do it."

"Not you," Dillon replied in a firm tone that offered no room for discussion. "Me."

Relieved, I nodded in agreement. I really hated heights.

"I think I should stay tonight," he said, a look of worry crossing his face. "I can sleep on the floor or the couch downstairs."

"No, I'll be fine," I argued. "Really. I don't think they can get out if the mirror is covered."

"I'll make certain the mirror is secure before I leave," Dillon said.

By now it was early evening with the sun setting fast. How would I be able to sleep with an evil spirit roaming inside the house?

I placed the bathrobe back over the mirror. For extra insurance Dillon anchored my shag rug over it, as well. Then we closed the closet door and made sure the latch clicked.

I followed Dillon downstairs and then out of the house through the mud room. He had grown up on a farm, so he had no trouble starting the tractor and positioning the wagon below my window.

The fact that neither of my parents seemed to have heard the tractor being moved was proof of how big that old house was. We only hoped we could get this done before anyone questioned us. Dad left for work on the other side of the house, while Mom still worked from home. We hoped no one would venture out to find a tractor and a wagon parked in front of the hostas and the daylilies.

Dillon assured me he would be back here bright and early in the morning. He talked about it as if it were a secret mission.

As the last slice of sunlight slanted across the driveway, I walked Dillon to his car.

He paused, looking up at my bedroom window. "Are you okay leaving the window open?"

"Sure," I said with the wave of a hand. "No one's going to walk in through a third story window."

He gave me a sweet kiss. Then crawled into his car and drove away.

I turned and stared up at my dark window. It really didn't look any different from down here, but I knew it was. From this perspective the hay wagon looked like it was parked there just waiting to be driven back to the barn.

Exhausted, I made the climb to my third story bedroom. Skipping my nightly bubble bath, I found comfort in my soft canopy bed. My regular pillow was still damp, so I switched it with another one and buried my face in the softness.

It wasn't long before I felt myself drifting into sleep.

* * *

FOR some reason the Grandfather clock in the foyer woke me at the stroke of three. Normally, I slept right through the hourly chimes.

I rubbed my eyes and reached for my phone. It slipped from my fingers and landed on the floor. I reached over the side of the bed, fumbling for it. It flipped over under my searching fingers. Then several beeping sounds echoed.

The phone gave off just enough light for me to see a figure standing at the end of my bed.

It was Benjamin Kotter.

Terrified, I curled up against my headboard. "How did you get out?"

Quiet, eerie laughter filled my room. *"Yours is not the only full length mirror in this house,"* Kotter taunted.

How could I have been so stupid? Mom had ordered a full-length mirror almost identical to mine for her bathroom. It must have just arrived. That had to be how he got out.

"I felt mutiny in the air," he said with a snarl. *"Whatever you and that boy have planned, forget it. I have no intention of leaving this house."*

Kotter knew we were planning to get rid of him, but it seemed he didn't know how we were going to do it.

Dillon's voice echoed from the phone. I must have accidently hit redial when grabbing for the phone.

"Help me!" I shouted into the air. "He's here!"

"There is no one here to help you. No parents, no boy, no one." Kotter started toward me. *"This is where it ends for you, Molly Greyson."*

I jumped off the bed and scooped up my phone in the process.

"Jump, Molly!" Dillon screamed through the speaker.

Without hesitation, I stood in front of the tapestry. My knees shook with fear.

Kotter floated slowly toward me. The closer he came, the colder the air turned. Hatred seemed to be building within his dark wicked eyes. Then something came up behind Kotter. It pulled him away from me and tossed him across the room.

It was another ghost. It was Molly.

Outraged, Kotter turned and attacked Molly, shoving her across the floor and into the closet. With a flick of his wrist the door slammed shut, trapping Molly inside.

Then he turned with vengeance in his black eyes and flew toward me at great speed. I braced for impact.

As Kotter wrapped his icy grasp around me, I jumped backward with all my strength toward the window. The force of my weight pulled the tapestry from the wall. I fell out the window with Kotter on top of me. The tapestry floated beneath us like a magic carpet.

I hit the hay hard, landing flat on my back.

The chilling grip of ghostly hands slipped off my waist.

I opened my eyes to see a white vaporous figure floating into the dark night sky above me.

"What have you done, you wretched girl?" Kotter said, as his vaporous form began to fade.

I glanced up and saw Molly looking out the window at me.

Lights sped up the driveway. With the squeal of brakes, a car skidded to a stop.

A few seconds later Dillon vaulted into the wagon, setting up a spray of hay and making the old springs creak.

"Molly, are you alright?" Dillon looked me over and then brushed hay off my face. "I got here as fast as I could. What happened?"

"I'll be alright," I said. "I just need to catch my breath."

Dillon lay on his back beside me, and we both stared up at the star spattered sky.

A white vaporous figure hung high above us.

"Is that who I think it is?" Dillon asked, as the figure disappeared into the darkness.

"Yes, it's Kotter." Then I pointed up to the figure looking out of my bedroom window. "And that's who saved me."

CHAPTER 23

SOMEHOW, the phone was still clutched in my hand.

Lying there in the prickly hay piled up in the wagon, I looked to see what time it was. Three-thirty. It felted like much more time had passed.

"Hungry?" I asked.

"Are you joking?" Sitting up, Dillon propped his arms on his knees. "You just eliminated an evil ghost all by yourself and all you can think about is eating?"

"I guess I worked up an appetite. Do you think you could whip up some pancakes?" Just for effect, I batted my eyelashes at him. "First, I want to check on Molly. She was the one who sent Kotter into a rage. He came at me with such force, that he knocked us out the window."

"But how did he get out?" Dillon asked. "You covered your mirror."

"He gave away his secret. I forgot that Mom purchased a full length mirror for her bathroom. He came through that one. He told me he sensed we were scheming against him and he decided to take care of me while I was alone. But I wasn't alone. Molly was there."

I held out a hand. "Help me out of here. Then let's hope someone forgot to lock the mud room door."

* * *

THANKFULLY, we did find the back door unlocked. Otherwise Dillon would have been looking for lock-picking tools.

We slipped into the house, locked the door behind us, and sneaked quietly up the back stairs.

When we walked into my room we found Molly sitting on my bed, untangling her hair with my brush.

"I saw Benjamin Kotter vaporize into the sky," she said in a wispy voice. *"He is gone, forever. Thank you Molly Greyson."*

"Don't thank me," I said, sitting next to her. "You're the one who made Kotter mad enough to attack me. Thank you for your help."

Dillon sat on the other side of her. "Molly, you were so brave to come after Kotter like that. I'm so grateful you were here."

"This is nice," Molly said. *"It has been so long since I have had any friends. If*

it is possible, I have a request. Well, actually two requests."

"Yes, just name it," I said.

This ghost had just saved my life. I would help her any way I could.

"First, can you help me find my parents?" she asked. *"They aren't here in this house with me. Can you bring them here?"*

"How can we bring them to you?" I gave a shrug. "We don't know where they are. I thought you said if a ghost goes outside they will no longer be able to re-enter."

"That is only if the ghost goes outside the house where they died," Molly explained. *"My parents did not die in this house."*

"We'll do whatever we can to reunite you and your parents," Dillon vowed. "But how?"

"Place your mirror in the house where they died," Molly instructed. *"They can enter the mirror just as I did. When they are inside, cover it securely. Then return the mirror to this house so we can be together again."*

"That sounds simple enough," I said. "What's your second request?"

"Search the house where they died for Kotter's journal," Molly said. *"Prove my parents did not die of natural causes. They were murdered, and so was I."*

It took me a moment to absorb what she had just said. I never really considered that Molly had been murdered. I assumed she died from some sort of disease at an early age. But how could she know her parents were murdered unless they were murdered in front of her?

"Who did this to you?" I asked. "Was it the same person who murdered your parents?"

"It is a long story," Molly said in a sad voice.

"Please tell us," Dillon said. "We need to know, so we can help you."

Nodding in agreement, I reached toward her hand. I couldn't hold her hand, but did feel her cool touch.

"Very well. I will tell you what happened. But I will need to start from the beginning." Molly stood and began to float back and forth slowly, as if pacing. *"Please know that much of this is from my mother's words. I was very young in the beginning. In 1875 when I was five years old, we moved here from Ohio. My father was a prominent architect. He designed and built this house. It was completed in 1876 and we moved in. His company was very successful and he drew other businesses here. It was not long before the people of the territory voted to become a town. They insisted it be called Greysontown in honor of my father, because of the financial assistance he had given them when they moved here.*

"There was one family living in the area when we moved here. The man's name was Benjamin Kotter. He was a farmer, but he seemed to have a good financial head. It wasn't long before my father opened the Savings and Loan Company of

Greysontown and hired him to be in charge. My father's business was thriving and the town had become a popular place to live outside of Indianapolis. Then my father's business began to lose money. Several of the other businesses suffered the same financial trouble. The shop owners had no choice but to sell or lose everything. Benjamin Kotter started buying businesses and hiring the original owners to run them. When my father's architectural business took a turn toward bankruptcy, he hired a lawyer with his last money in savings to find out what was happening in Greysontown.

"The lawyer found out that Benjamin Kotter had been embezzling money from all the businesses that had money in the Savings and Loan. My father was also one of the victims. He planned to turn him in with the proof his lawyer had uncovered and expose him for the thief he was. My father invited Benjamin Kotter to our house on April 10. He also invited his lawyer and the local Constable to attend the meeting, so he could be arrested on the spot and taken to jail once the issue was exposed. The year was 1886. I was sixteen.

"Mother and I were in the ballroom fitting my dress for the upcoming cotillion. Father was there with us, waiting for Benjamin to arrive. George, our butler, first brought the lawyer and then Benjamin into the ballroom where we were. I remember my father asking George if any other visitors had arrived. Assuming the Constable had been delayed but was on his way, my father began the conversation. Mother and I stood to the side and allowed the men to talk. It was not long before voices were raised and Mother tried to take me out of the ballroom. Benjamin ordered her to stop. He pulled a pistol from his jacket. The gun fired, hitting me in the chest. My father was so distraught he jumped on Benjamin and the gun went off again. My father dropped to his knees bleeding from his stomach. My mother held me in her arms, as Benjamin turned another pistol on the lawyer, shooting him in the head.

"The last thing I remember was the Constable entering the ballroom and Benjamin ordering him to take my mother and father to his house where he would finish the task. The Constable had another officer drag my bleeding father out of the room, while he pulled my mother from me. She was kicking and screaming as she reached for me. He asked Benjamin what to do with me. Benjamin's reply was: 'Leave her. She's not long for this world anyway. I'll take care of her body later.' I remember every word, as if he had just spoken them. I died in the ballroom that day, alone."

Molly fell silent and sat on the floor in front of us.

I went over and tried to put my arms around her but it was impossible to hug her. I couldn't imagine the pain she had gone through or was suffering right now re-telling the story.

Dillon had not said a word or moved from his spot on the bed. He looked like he was in shock.

"If you died in the ballroom," I asked after a few minutes, "how do you know where Kotter took your parents and that he murdered them?"

"I did not find out until Benjamin Kotter died and joined this existence," Molly explained. *"When he found me roaming between the walls of this house, he bragged about taking my parents to his house and shooting them. He believed in the afterlife and did not want my parents to be with me. That is why he had them taken to his house and shot. He wanted them to suffer even in this realm."*

I thought about what Dillon and I had found in the archives. The dates just didn't add up.

"But we found proof that your father signed over the estate to Kotter on April 27, 1886," I said. "You just told us that he murdered all of you on April 10. How can that be?"

"Benjamin Kotter had been forging signatures for years on documents, so that he could embezzle money," Molly answered. *"He had nearly every Constable and lawyer in Greysontown on his payroll. That is why the Constable my father asked to come never showed up. The lawyer my father hired was from Ohio, so he wasn't involved in the conspiracy. Shortly after our disappearance, Benjamin moved into this house. I tried my best to intrude into his life, but I was a new entity and had no skills. Not long after moving into the estate, he appointed himself the Town Commissioner and changed the town's name to Kottersville. No one opposed him for fear of threats to their families and businesses. The name Greysontown was never to be spoken again. How do I know all these things if I died before Benjamin? He unveiled everything to me once he became as me. He gloated about his tyranny and ability to control everyone. And he was controlling me even then."*

"Do you know how Kotter died?" Dillon asked.

"Yes, I know how he died." A look of pride crossed her ghostly features. *"I killed him."*

Dillon and I gasped at the same time.

"I worked on my skills over the years, watching his moves as he wandered around the house," Molly explained. *"I was waiting for an opportune moment. One day Benjamin was in the ballroom hanging photos of the long ago gala events held in this house, when he went over to the elevator. He was not in good health and had declined even more since his wife passed the year before of a heart attack while pruning roses outside. He grew more and more distraught every day and paid no attention to his health. He was leaving the ballroom on the elevator and happened to pull the gates open prematurely before the elevator arrived. I had found my way out of the walls years before when I found that I was able to roam freely by going through the dressing mirror in his daughter's bedroom. I had been following him around, waiting for a situation such as this. Before he knew what was happening I flew across the room and with all the force I could build I shoved him into the elevator shaft. The elevator had just started to ascend and he landed nearly three floors down on top of the elevator. It continued to rise and pinned him between the ceiling and the elevator roof. It was a*

week before anyone came to look for him and another day before they found him. By then he was with me and he was angry. Since then I have stayed as far away from him as possible. I tried to make contact with the living who resided here, but Benjamin always found a way to keep me away and run them out. The house had been vacant for such a long time before you arrived. But there was something extraordinary about you. Now I know that special feeling was our biological bond."

I sat there, speechless. She had waited decades to kill Kotter and finally succeeded. But she didn't stop to think that would put him in her world where she would have to deal with his rage. Now she was rid of him and she could be free. We had to find her parents and bring them to her. She deserved happiness even as a ghost.

"Molly," I began, "you said you know where Kotter took your parents. Can you tell us the address?"

"Yes," Molly replied. *"Benjamin's old house at 897 Hollyhock Lane."*

I looked at Dillon. "Where is 897 Hollyhock Lane?"

His face turned a dull shade of gray, and then he cleared his throat. "It's my address. The street name was changed to Darby Lane, when we turned the house into a B&B years ago. I—I have ghosts in my house."

Silence shrouded the room.

CHAPTER 24

"OKAY, everyone stay calm," I said with my heart racing.

"I'm going to need to tell my mom about this," Dillon said.

"Not just yet. Let's do what Molly asked. Then we'll fill everyone in, including my parents." I turned to Molly. "Why would an attic access door be sealed over with bricks? It can't keep ghosts locked inside."

"It was a custom in the early 1800's to brick over any access to lower levels or upper levels of a house that had been deemed haunted by the un-living," Molly explained. *"I know now that was just a myth. However, a ghost did need to find ways to transport out of the walls. Thus a mirror."*

There was one question I hated to ask, but we needed to know.

"Molly, where is your grave?"

"I do not have a real grave," Molly replied. *"Benjamin buried me in the basement. Then he built a brick wall to cover any evidence and to, what he believed, keep me in. But as you know now that was not successful. He did make some crude gravestones, but instead of placing them anywhere he threw them in the hole with me. Over the years the bricks crumbled and his crime was left to be exposed, except no one ever went down into the basement to find the stones. That's why he ran all prior tenants off the property, to protect his secret."*

"So that's what I saw in the basement," Dillon interjected. "I was right. They were gravestones."

Molly's bones were still buried in the basement? I shuddered at the thought and knew we had to rectify that.

"Tell us about this journal of Kotter's," I said. "Do you know where it's hidden?"

"All I know is Benjamin bragged that he wrote everything in a journal and had it well hidden in the old house. I did detect some worry that he had not had time to retrieve it before his death. I am certain it is still hidden at the old house." Molly looked at Dillon. *"At his house."*

"Okay." I turned to Dillon. "If you're ready, I am."

He jumped off the bed and lifted me up from the floor, where I had been sitting next to Molly.

"Let's go," he said. "We have a lot of work to do in a small amount of time. School starts in two days. The sooner we solve this mystery, the better. I just need to find a delicate way to tell my mom."

"Molly," I said, "you don't have to go back into the mirror. You can stay out and enjoy your freedom from Kotter. He won't be able to control you anymore." I spied the purple dress on my chair. "The dress is yours. It always was."

With a smile, she turned her head toward the dress.

* * *

DILLON made a quick trip across town and back to swap his car for an old truck his Mom kept around the B&B for hauling things.

Then he met me back upstairs. With great care he hauled my mirror down the back stairway, through the kitchen, and out the mud room door. Using all those magnificent muscles, he loaded the mirror into the bed of the truck and covered it with a tarp.

On the way through the kitchen, I grabbed a couple of donuts off the counter and pulled two bottles of orange juice out of the fridge. I hurried out the back door and climbed into the passenger side of the truck.

Dillon started the engine and sped down the driveway. After pulling onto the highway, he grabbed one of the donuts and took a big bite. "How are we going to explain the mirror to Mom?" He finished the donut and then took a big swig of orange juice.

"We have to be honest," I replied. "Just tell her we're going to use it to get two ghosts out of your house and take them back to my house."

Dillon choked on his orange juice. "Just like that? *Ignore the mirror, Mom. It's only a ghost extraction. Nothing to worry about.* Are you serious?"

"No silly," I said, licking donut sugar from my fingers. "She needs to be there when we contact Molly's parents. That way she will have to believe. It's the right thing to do."

"Well, that sounds simple," Dillon replied, eyes on the road. "But there's one problem. Mom is pretty adamant about staying away from that bricked up attic access."

"Let me handle it," I offered, feeling confident. "I think I have a solution."

There were only a couple cars in the Bed and Breakfast parking lot when we arrived.

Dillon backed the truck close to the rear entrance. We unloaded the mirror and very carefully hauled it up the back stairs, which were used mainly for deliveries and maintenance.

We could hear his mom's voice, as she visited with guests.

Before we were spotted, we hurried into his old room and placed the mirror on the floor. He pushed the wardrobe away from the closet door like it was made of packing foam. Then we slid the mirror into the closet and positioned it in front of the attic access door.

"Okay, let's go get your mom." I felt a frisson of hesitation.

"After you," Dillon said. "Maybe I should slip a sedative in Mom's coffee first."

He gave a lop-sided grin. I hoped he was joking.

By the time we got to the front desk, Dillon's mom had just finished checking in her new guests.

"Mom," Dillon began, "Molly and I need you to come upstairs with us. We have something to show you. It's a surprise."

Boy, was that an understatement!

His mom closed the guestbook and looked up with a smile. "What's this all about? A surprise? I hope it's a good one."

She followed us upstairs, but balked when we stopped in front his old bedroom. "Why are we going in there?" she asked, no longer smiling.

"Trust me, Mom," Dillon said, taking her arm. "You need to see this with your own eyes."

"Wait." She pulled her arm out of Dillon's grip. "Does this have something to do with your dad's things in the attic?"

"No," Dillon reassured her, shaking his head. "It has nothing to do with Dad's things. It's something entirely different."

Dillon again secured his mom's arm and guided her into the room. When she saw the wardrobe pushed to one side and the closet door opened, she backed away.

"I can't," she said, shaking her head. "I thought we were clear on this, Dillon."

"Please, Mom. We need you to see this, so you will understand."

She spotted the mirror in the closet. "What's that mirror doing in here? It was never here before."

I stepped in front of the mirror, while Dillon and his mom stood behind me.

"Mr. and Mrs. Greyson," I called softly. I didn't expect them to pop up instantly, so I continued. "I am here on behalf of your daughter, Molly. She has sent us here to contact you, so that you can be reunited with her at your estate."

I looked at the reflection of Dillon's mom in the mirror. She had a mix of sheer terror and confusion on her face.

When I looked back into the mirror, two faces appeared followed by their full figures. I recognized them from the old photos.

"Hello," I said in a shaky voice. "I am a descendent of the Greyson family. My name is Molly Greyson, just like your daughter. She still exists at Greyson Estate and has requested our help in transporting you in this mirror back to the estate to be with her."

I saw Dillon grab his mom. She looked about ready to faint.

"Mom, take a deep breath," Dillon advised. "I know this is a lot to take in without warning. But you have to believe this to be true. The only way is to be right here right now while it's happening."

"How is it that Molly knew where we were?" Mr. Greyson asked. *"Benjamin Kotter killed my daughter at the estate. Then he brought us to this house and murdered us."*

"Kotter died at the estate," I explained. "When he joined Molly in the afterworld, he gloated about what he had done to you at his old house. We were able to cleanse the estate of his presence. Now she needs you to come back home and be with her. All you have to do is stay right there in the mirror and we will do the rest."

The two ghosts looked at each other, looked back at me, and then nodded in unison.

At that point, Dillon's mom fainted. He caught her before she hit the ground. With a little maneuvering, he carried her out of the closet and then laid her on the bed. Grabbing a magazine from the night stand, he fanned her face. In a moment, she opened her eyes. He pulled the juice bottle out of his jeans pocket and offered it to her. She drank the remainder in one huge gulp.

"Feeling a bit better now?" he asked.

"Dillon, you're right," his mom stated. "If I had not seen it with my own eyes, I would never have believed it. My word, there are ghosts in our house!" She paused, and her brows furrowed. "It wasn't your dad's ghost in the attic? It was the ghosts of two people murdered in this house? The Greyson's? They're relatives of yours, Molly?"

"Yes," I replied. "It's a long story, one we can tell you later. But we have one more thing we need to ask."

Mrs. Darby's head dropped to her chest, as if she dreaded the request.

"We are looking for something that was owned by Benjamin Kotter. Molly said it was hidden somewhere in this house." I paused to give her a moment to think. "May we take down the brick wall and go into the attic to search for it?"

Mrs. Darby's face filled with relief. "It won't be necessary to tear down the brick wall. All that is up there are things left from Dillon's dad.

Before the bricks were put in, I removed everything else. I found several boxes in the attic filled with documents, books, and ledgers from the previous owner. I placed them in the back of the garage and forgot about them. Is that what you're looking for?"

"Possibly," Dillon said. "Do you remember seeing a leather bound journal in any of the boxes?"

Dillon's mom seemed to be searching her memories. "No, not really, but you can look for yourselves."

"Mom, did you know that this was the original Kotter house when you bought it?"

His mom hesitated before answering, as if to collect her thoughts. "Not at the time your dad and I purchased the house. It wasn't until I decided to make it into a Bed and Breakfast did I find out who the builder and original owner was. It was something to do with legal mumbo-jumbo and deeds and the like. By then Kotter was dead, and I didn't see a need to tell you. Besides, I didn't think it mattered to you who owned this house before us. Now it matters considerably since Kotter murdered those people here. I'm just not certain anyone will take the word of ghosts. I had no idea that any of the Greyson's relatives lived in this town. Is there any way to prove any of this?"

Dillon nodded and looked a bit sheepish. "As a matter of fact, there is. Molly and I 'borrowed' some information from the town archives. Kotter may not be here to pay for his crime, but it will help set things right for the Greyson family. If we can find that journal."

I looked over my shoulder at the two figures in the mirror. They seemed to be waiting patiently, while we sorted through the mess of information.

"Before we can do that, we have a job to complete," I interjected. "We need to get the mirror with Molly's parents back to my house. Then we can deal with the lost journal."

"You're right," Dillon said. "We need to get the Greyson's back with Molly. Then we need to tell your parents."

I opened my mouth to protest, but he raised a finger to stop me.

"If Mom will come with us, it won't be such a shock for them," he explained.

Actually, that sounded like a very logical solution.

"I'll go," Mrs. Darby said. "But can I drive myself? I don't think I can ride in the same truck with the—the mirror."

"Really, Mom," Dillon said with a chuckle. "You've being living with the Greyson's all these years. It's about time you got to know them."

"Molly said to place a blanket over the mirror," I explained to the Greyson's, watching me from within the glass. "I'm sorry. I have to cover you up. It won't be for very long."

I pulled a blanket down from the shelf and placed it over the mirror, making certain it covered the glass. Using a rope we had brought with us, I secured the blanket at the bottom of the frame.

A terrifying thought popped into my brain. If we broke the mirror, would the Greyson's be lost in another realm, unable to reunite with their daughter?

I reached out and put a firm hold on Dillon's arm, causing him to look up at me. "Please don't drop it."

He flashed a confident smile. "Not a chance. Now guide me down the stairs."

* * *

WITH the mirror secured in the bed of the truck, Dillon pulled out of the B&B parking lot and onto the street.

As Dillon drove, I braced one hand against the passenger side dashboard and watched through the rear window to make sure the blanket remained over the mirror.

Dillon's mom followed close behind in the car.

We pulled up to a stop light and saw Dillon's basketball buddy, Clay, standing on the corner.

Clay came over to the truck. "Whatcha haulin', dude?" He looked into the truck bed and reached down to lift up the blanket.

Just then the light turned green. Dillon hit the accelerator. With tires squealing, he pulled away from Clay's grasping hands.

I looked back and saw Clay standing in the street with a dumb expression on his face.

"You're going to have some explaining to do when you talk to Clay at your next practice," I said.

Dillon just shrugged.

A few minutes later we made the last curve of the long driveway up to my house. Dillon drove to the back entrance and stopped the truck.

"How are we going to get the mirror inside?" Dillon asked. "Your dad's car is in the garage. That means he's home."

"Leave that to me," I said.

I hopped out of the truck, just as Dillon's mom pulled up out front. I ran to her car and asked her to ring the door chimes to distract my parents. His mom seemed nervous, but agreed to help.

When I heard the chimes, I knew Mrs. Darby was at the front door. I motioned to Dillon and then ran to help him.

As we pulled the mirror out of the truck the blanket got caught on one of the bolts and it began to slip off. Frantic, I jumped on the fender. I loosened the blanket from the bolt and then re-tied it at the bottom.

Dillon eased the mirror out the truck bed and headed straight for the back door.

We covered two flights of stairs as quickly and quietly as possible. The stairs that led to my third floor bedroom were on the other end of a long hallway past the ballroom.

"Hey, kids," Mom called from inside the ballroom. "What do you have there?"

Startled, I tripped on the blanket, causing it to drop to the floor. As I scrambled to grab the blanket, I lost my grip on the mirror. Dillon fought to hold up his end, but it was too late.

The mirror hit the floor with a deafening crack. Then smaller tinkling sounds echoed, as a million shards of glass hit the wood floor.

There was a poof of vaporous cold air. Then two figures emerged from the broken mirror.

Mom walked out of the ballroom. Her eyes grew round and wide. She slapped both hands over her mouth, presumably to stifle a scream.

The two ghostly figures hovered just above the floor next to me.

Then Dad came running down the hall toward us from the direction of my bedroom. He stopped short, skidding on the long hallway rug.

Mrs. Darby raced up the main stairs and stopped by Dillon's side.

Time seemed to stop.

Everyone stood there motionless in an eerie silence.

I looked at Dillon, who gave a defeated shrug.

Well, there it was. Time for the truth.

"Mom, Dad," I began. "This is Mr. and Mrs. Greyson." I waited for the explosion.

Mom tumbled over in a faint, and Dad raced to catch her. He crumpled up under her and sat down hard on the floor.

Mrs. Darby surveyed the broken mirror on the floor and seemed to understand what had happened. At least she had been somewhat prepared for this. My poor parents had no clue.

Molly heard the commotion and floated toward us from my bedroom. She saw her parents and they immediately embraced each other. Their faces showed genuine emotion, but there were no tears.

Mom opened her eyes at that moment, gave a strangled little shriek, and fainted again. She fell back into Dad's arms like a sack of potatoes.

When Mrs. Darby began to cry, Dillon comforted her.

I stood alone, watching everything unfold around me.

Molly came over to me and held out her hand. I placed my hand into her icy touch.

"Thanks to Molly and Dillon," she said. *"I have my parents back where they belong."*

Mom was now fully awake. With Dad's help, she got to her feet.

"Young lady," Mom said in a voice that matched the stern expression on her face, "you have some explaining to do."

CHAPTER 25

DAD was able to get Mom down to the living room and settled on the couch. Dillon and his mom joined them, while I went to ask Tilly to make us some coffee.

Then I ran upstairs to the ballroom, where Molly and her parents were still enjoying their reunion.

"Sorry to intrude," I said. "But can I ask a huge favor?"

"Anything for you my dear," Laura Greyson said. *"You have given us such a gift. How can we repay you?"*

"Would you help me explain things to my parents?" I asked. "If we're going to co-exist here, they need to know the whole story. Molly has already told Dillon and me what she knows. I need your help in filling in the gaps. And talking to our parents."

"Yes, of course," Mr. Greyson said.

The three of them left the ballroom. I followed them down the front stairs and into the main room.

Tilly had already served coffee and brought in fresh made cookies. I grabbed a cookie and shoved it in my mouth. Chocolate chip cookies always made things better.

As the three ghosts floated into the room, Mom burrowed deeper into the couch cushions and curled her legs underneath her. Dad sat beside her, rigid as a statue. Mrs. Darby seemed remarkably relaxed.

Tilly turned white as a sheet. The silver coffee server dropped from her hand. It hit the floor with a loud clang, and hot coffee ran in a round puddle at her feet. "I—I—I'm sorry, Mrs. Greyson. I thought I saw—" She gulped. "Ghosts," she said in a strangled whisper.

Mom hopped up from the couch and grabbed Tilly by the arm. "It's alright."

The ghostly Mrs. Greyson floated to them. *"I didn't mean to alarm you,"* she said in a gentle voice.

Both Mrs. Greyson's, my mom and Molly's mom, stood face-to-face.

Tilly looked back and forth at them, as if watching a tennis match.

Molly's mom smiled at my mom. *"I believe this might get a bit confusing, as we are both Mrs. Greyson."*

How would Mom react? Faint? Run screaming from the room?
Neither. She laughed.

"Yes," Mom said. "I can see where this might cause some confusion.
My first name is Lara. And yours?"

Mrs. Greyson laughed, covering her mouth in Victorian era fashion.
"My name is Laura, also."

"But Mom," I chimed in, "your name is spelled L-A-R-A and her
name is spelled L-A-U-R-A."

Mom scowled as though I had interrupted some kind of adult
moment, so I sat down next to Dillon.

"What else do you know about all this?" Dad asked in a stern voice.
"From the looks of things, I'd say you have known about the ghosts—"
He paused to clear his throat. "I mean, the Greyson's for a while now.
Why haven't you told us?"

I wanted to hit rewind and rethink this entire meeting of the two
generations, but it was too late. Time to come clean.

"Well," I started slowly, "I have known about Molly for a couple
days. It wasn't until right before you met them, that I also met the
Greyson's."

Dad's face pulled into a serious scowl.

"Mr. Greyson's name is also William," I said. "Like you, Dad."

Dad's sour expression morphed into one of puzzlement. "We all
three have the same names? I somehow feel very left out of the loop
right now. Would you mind doing some major explaining, little lady?"

Oh, great. The 'little lady' comment. Dad never used that unless he
was angry.

"Possibly," Mr. Greyson interceded on my behalf, *"it might be more
accurate if my wife and I explained the circumstances of how we happened to end up as
entities in this house."*

Dad's attention shifted to the ghostly Mr. Greyson. "Yes, of course.
Please. I want nothing more than to understand what is happening here."

Dillon and I sat with our mouths firmly closed and allowed Mr.
Greyson to tell their story.

As we listened, we nodded on what facts Molly had shared with us.
Mr. Greyson was able to confirm all that Molly had told us about Kotter
plus add some critical points Molly had not known.

When the tale was finished, my dad stood and walked around the
room. He called it his 'physical thinking'. I knew he was just trying to
digest the facts.

"So," Dad mused, obviously still in thinking mode, "in a nut shell, you built this house and lived here for ten years. Benjamin Kotter had already started to embezzle money from the Savings and Loan Company which he was in charge of. When the business owners were told they were losing money, that's when Kotter swooped in and took over the companies." Dad paused for a moment. More thinking, apparently. "Because you didn't want to relinquish your family architecture company, he bargained with you and ended up with this house."

"No, I never signed this house over to him," Mr. Greyson corrected. *"He murdered all three of us before that happened and somehow he ended up with the house. The only one left of our family was our son, Matthew, who lived in Chicago with his wife and son. Because Kotter owned all the lawyers in town he was able to get papers drawn up and get the house placed in his hands before Matthew was able to do anything about it."*

"Wait!" I interrupted. "I believe Dillon and I know how Kotter took over the house for himself. Molly told us he bragged that he had been forging signatures for years to get what he wanted. He forged your signature after your death, Mr. Greyson, and we can prove it."

After running upstairs to my bedroom, I grabbed the information Dillon and I had 'borrowed' from the town archives, and then thumped back downstairs.

Breathless, I slammed the folder down on the coffee table and everyone gathered around me.

"This is a copy of the deed to this house," I said. "See the date? It's dated April 27, 1886, and supposedly signed by both William A. Greyson and Benjamin Kotter. Molly told us that it was on April 10, 1886 that Kotter came to the house and met with her father in the ballroom. It was on that day her mother was fitting her for her cotillion dress. And it was on that day she and her parents were murdered. Mr. Greyson couldn't have signed the deed. He was already dead." I stopped and took a long breath. "It also says it was sold for an undisclosed amount, which means he literally stole the house."

"May I examine this document more closely?" Mr. Greyson asked. *"I believe I heard you read my name incorrectly."*

We all waited in anticipation for Mr. Greyson to read over the document. It wasn't long before he lowered the paper and smiled.

"Ah," Mr Greyson said. *"This is most definitely a forgery, and I will help you prove it. My middle name is Orwell. William Orwell Greyson. Somehow Kotter mistook my O as an A when forging my name and no one caught it. The deed is null and void and should revert back to the original owners. Which in this case is you, William, my great-grandson."*

Dad's stern expression melted when Mr. Greyson called him great-grandson. "Molly, I'm not even going to ask how or why you got this folder, but I am very glad you did. I believe we need to take a trip to the Town Hall and rectify this situation immediately."

Then I realized that it was the Gypsy who prompted me to do some digging into the Kotter estate. But what did the Gypsy have to do with any of this? She wasn't real. Someone had to be behind this.

My brain was so fried at the moment I couldn't begin another search for the person responsible for the Gypsy. School started in two days. After that, maybe things would fall into a more normal routine. Well, as normal as it could be with ghosts and humans sharing the same house.

I heard Dad on the phone talking to his attorney. He wasn't kidding about setting the records straight immediately.

"It's all arranged," Dad said, after the call ended. "My attorney will meet us at the Town Hall. We'll get the legal paperwork started to get this situation set right."

Dad offered a hand to Mr. Greyson. He gladly responded by reaching out his hand to Dad. I was impressed that Dad only flinched a little when his warm hand met what I knew from experience was an icy patch of air. Dad was very macho about it.

I looked around for Dillon. He was gone. I searched the kitchen and spied Dillon and his mom outside by her car.

"Are you leaving so soon Mrs. Darby?" I asked, a bit worried.

"She wants to go to the Town Hall with us," Dillon answered, "and do some investigating of her own."

* * *

DAD'S attorney was waiting for us when we arrived at the Town Hall. He had wasted no time getting here from Indianapolis. I had ridden there with my parents to give Dillon and his mom some privacy.

When we walked in, Mrs. Hill was sitting behind her desk as usual. She raised her head to greet the new visitors and was stunned to see me and Dillon. Her bubbly smile morphed into a sneer.

"The Greyson's and I need to see the Town Manager right away," Dad's attorney said with authority. "We don't have an appointment, but this matter cannot wait."

Mrs. Hill did not mess with Dad's attorney. She picked up the phone and announced to the Town Manager that we were here requesting an immediate meeting. She nodded without answering and placed the phone on the hook. She pressed a buzzer under her desk and the small door swung open, allowing us entry into her perfectly organized domain.

"Mr. Wilson will see you now," she said through gritted teeth and then gave a tight smile. "But the children must stay here."

"Molly, you and Dillon wait with Mrs. Darby," Dad said winking at his attorney. "This won't take long."

I handed the folder and microfilm to Dad, and then he went through the small door. I saw Mrs. Hill eyeballing the items as he passed her.

"Isn't that—" Mrs. Hill stopped midsentence, when the Manager's door shut in her face.

I knew she recognized the folder and microfilm. She tossed a nasty look my way and then turned to Dillon's mom.

"How are you today, Mrs. Darby?" Mrs. Hill asked in a sugary voice. "What brings you down to the Town Hall?"

"I need to do a bit of research on my house," Mrs. Darby answered. "Would you mind if we search the basement for a certain file?"

Mrs. Hill's shoulders twitched. "If it's something I can help you with, I'll be most happy to do so. But the children will not be allowed to join you in the archives."

"And why is that, Mrs. Hill?" Mrs. Darby questioned.

Mrs. Hill might suspect that Dillon and I had done something wrong, but we knew she couldn't prove it.

"Well, I guess if the guard accompanies you, it won't be a problem," Mrs. Hill grumbled. She hobbled over to the door and unlocked it with a key. Then she motioned for the guard. "Please try to hurry. My lunch hour begins in thirty minutes."

"If I find the right documents, it won't take long at all," Mrs. Darby reassured her.

I couldn't imagine what Mrs. Darby was looking for, but I followed close behind her if for no other reason than to get away from Mrs. Hill. Dillon dogged my heels and the guard trailed along behind him. It had turned into quite a little parade.

"Just what are we looking for?" Dillon asked his Mom. "The deed to the house?"

"No, not the deed," Mrs. Darby replied in a quiet voice. "I'm looking for the Darby family records. I want to verify something."

"That would be in the personal records section," Dillon said.

He walked to the far side of the room with everyone following him, including the guard. Dillon found the drawer marked DAB-DUT and pulled it open. It wasn't long before he found the Darby folder and handed it to his mom.

"Let's take this over to the table where there's better lighting," Mrs. Darby said.

She sat in the nearest chair and opened the folder. Flipping through page after page, she ran her fingers down each column. "What I'm looking for isn't here. I need to look at the Kollen records."

"Kollen is my mom's maiden name," Dillon whispered and then headed toward the correct cabinet.

Dillon found the folder without any problem and laid it down in front of his mom. She repeated the process of flipping pages and reading names like she was on a mission.

Suddenly, she stopped. "Jacob Kollen," she read out loud. "Dillon, can you pull up the Kotter file?"

With a look of confusion, Dillon returned to the cabinets and soon found the Kotter file. He laid it in front of his mom. She opened the file and searched it like the previous ones. In a moment, her finger stopped on another name.

"Jacob Kotter and Jacob Kollen is the same person," she announced. "His name was misspelled when the files were transcribed."

"But Kollen was your maiden name," Dillon said. "How can you be a Kotter?"

"All of the names, including his, in this file are in my family bible," Mrs. Darby sat back in the chair and heaved a great sigh. "It says here his father was Benjamin Kotter. Dillon, we're the descendants of Benjamin Kotter."

"We're what?" Dillon sputtered. "There's got to be some mistake."

"Yes, a huge mistake," Mrs. Darby replied. "Whoever translated the old records must have not been able to read the handwriting and misspelled the name. The mistake continued on birth records, death records, and even marriage licenses."

"So you're telling me that Benjamin Kotter was my great-great-grandfather?" Dillon looked shaken. "No, that can't be right."

"All the old records were handwritten," his mom explained. "It's easy to see how Kotter became Kollen. You heard what Mr. Greyson said about the fake signature on the deed. Kotter translated an O for an A. That's the loophole William's attorney is using to void the document."

"Let me see if I have this straight," Dillon said, taking a deep breath. "I am just now finding out that my great-great-grandfather is Benjamin Kotter." He pointed at me. "The one who murdered Molly's great-great-grandparents and their daughter."

"Yes," I added, "but that also means my great-aunt murdered your great-great-grandfather."

Dillon stood there, looking disillusioned.

"I think we need to make copies of these documents," I said. "Let's take this to Mrs. Hill and ask her to run a few copies."

The guard escorted us upstairs and locked the door behind him.

"Mrs. Hill," Mrs. Darby asked, "would you be so kind as to run four copies of the pages in this folder?"

"I don't believe I can do that," Mrs. Hill replied, jutting out her chin in defiance.

Just then Mr. Wilson's door opened and out walked Dad and his attorney. They shook hands and were all smiles.

"Mrs. Hill, make certain these nice people get everything they need," Mr. Wilson said.

Mrs. Hill's face turned beet red and for a moment it looked like she might explode. "Yes, Mr. Wilson," she said through clenched teeth. "I'll see what I can do to be of assistance."

"The copies my mom requested," Dillon said. "If you don't mind."

He held the folder in front of Mrs. Hill. She grabbed the papers and then stomped off to make copies. I swear I saw steam coming off the top of her head.

"Well," Dad said to his attorney, "I believe everything is in order. Now it's just a matter of signing a few papers and we'll be the legitimate owners of Greyson Estate once again." He turned to Dillon's mom. "Did you get what you needed, Mrs. Darby?"

Mrs. Hill slapped the requested copies on the counter.

Dillon scooped them up before the old woman changed her mind.

"Yes," Mrs. Darby said. "I believe we have everything we need now."

* * *

WHEN we arrived back at my house, Tilly had an apple pie still warm from the oven and fresh coffee.

Passing on the coffee, I poured me and Dillon large glasses of milk. Everyone sat together at the large dining table and began discussing the latest events, while enjoying hot apple pie. Even the Greyson's and Molly sat with us.

I noticed Mrs. Darby was picking at her piece of pie.

"Dillon," I said in a quiet voice, leaning close to him. "I think your mom needs to tell my parents what she found at Town Hall."

Dillon nodded. He went over and whispered in his mom's ear. I saw her shake her head 'no' at first. Then after a bit more quiet discussion, she nodded.

Mrs. Darby cleared her throat. "Excuse me. I hate to rain on this celebration, but I have news that might be of interest."

The room grew quiet. All eyes, living and ghost, turned toward her.

With shaking hands, Mrs. Darby pulled the copies from her purse. "While you were in the Town Manager's office, I did some investigating of my own. I decided to look up my family history. It seems there was a big mistake made decades ago on my side of the family. My maiden name was Kollen. Or rather, I thought it was Kollen until today. After looking at my family records, I saw that after my great-grandfather died someone had miss-read the name and wrote it as Kollen. From then on all family members were Kollen's." Tears streamed down her face. "It seems my maiden name was Kotter. I'm Benjamin Kotter's great-granddaughter."

Everyone looked stunned.

"Emily," Dad said in a calm and reassuring voice, "you bear no blame for that."

Dad's attorney asked to see the copies. "Every document has to have the recorder's name on the final copy," the lawyer explained, after a few minutes. "It says here that the recorder was Donald Sunman. I'll do some checking and see if I can come up with any connections to the Kotter family. Possibly, the recorder was also on the Kotter payroll to alter documents intentionally."

"You won't have to look very far," my dad said. "I think I know the family. John Sunman is our realtor."

I leaned over to Dillon. "That makes sense," I whispered in his ear. "He lied to us about the time between residents of the estate. He comes from a long line of liars."

After all of the information had been laid out, a more comfortable atmosphere settled in the room.

"Did the records list the names of Kotter's children?" I asked.

"Well, yes," Mrs. Darby answered. "His children were listed. I believe they were Benjamin II and Geraldine. Why?"

"Did you scan down the date of death column to see what was listed for them?" I asked.

"No." She looked a little confused. "I didn't check that column on any of the Kotter's."

"We did check it. It listed their deaths dates as 'unknown'." I looked over at the ghosts. "Molly, do you know what happened to Kotter's children?"

Molly lowered her head, as if in reverence. *"Yes, I know. Benjamin was becoming more and more paranoid every day. On one afternoon I recall an argument between him and his daughter, Geraldine. I believe it was over a boy who wished to court her. She stormed out of the house with Kotter following behind her. I observed them from a second story window as they continued the altercation outside. Kotter pulled a small handgun and shot Geraldine on the front lawn. That night I watched as he buried her where the barn now stands. That is why her ghost does not live here. She was killed outside."*

There were gasps all around the room.

"Do you know what happened to Benjamin II?" I asked.

"Mrs. Kotter sent her son to live with her aunt in Ohio," Molly replied. *"I believe she was afraid her son would meet with the same fate as her daughter."*

"Mrs. Kotter knew her husband killed their daughter?" I was shocked at the news.

"Yes, but she was in ill health," Molly informed. *"I could tell she was afraid of Kotter. He never allowed her to have any visitors. She died of a heart attack in the garden. That is why her ghost does not roam these halls."*

An odd expression crossed Dillon's face. "We need to go back to the basement and look for the gravestones," he said.

"There is no need," Molly reported. *"I can confirm that the gravestone of my parents, Geraldine, and even mine is in the room in the basement. I watched Kotter throw them in when he was bricking up the wall."*

I sighed with relief knowing I didn't have to go on a gravestone hunting expedition in the basement.

"Dad, we think Molly is still buried in the basement," I informed. "And we're pretty sure there are gravestones down there with her. Would it be possible to create a cemetery somewhere private on the property?"

"Absolutely," Dad replied with a firm nod. "That is a wonderful idea, Molly. I will see to it."

Molly nodded her approval. I thought I actually saw a glisten of a single tear on her cheek.

CHAPTER 26

THE weekend after school started, I invited Emma and Autumn over for a slumber party.

I wanted to introduce them to Molly, but I wasn't certain how they would react. The evening started off with a huge pizza from the local pizzeria. I had even recorded a couple of great romance movies for the evening.

"I hope you don't mind," I said, after placing the empty pizza box on my desk, "but I invited another one of my friends to join us tonight."

"Is she from California?" Emma asked.

"No," I replied. "She lives here with me."

"How come we've never heard about her?" Autumn asked. "Well, bring her out. We want to meet her."

"Promise you'll be nice to her," I warned.

Autumn looked wounded. "Molly, why would you even ask that? Is there something wrong with her?"

"No, she's wonderful," I said.

It was now or never. I had prepared my friends—well, sort of prepared them for what was to come. I went over to the closet and opened the door.

Molly floated out next to me.

Autumn gasped.

Emma stared with her mouth wide open.

"Please be calm," I begged. "This is Molly. She is, um, well—"

"A ghost," Molly finished the sentence for me. *"My name is Molly. I live here at Greyson Estate with Molly and her family. Molly wanted us to meet so we could all be friends. I will not harm you. I am so happy to meet both of you. Molly has told me what good friends you have been to her."*

"But—but I don't believe in ghosts," Autumn squeaked.

"You might think about starting tonight," I said. "Molly is joining our slumber party."

"The rumors are true then," Emma added with a nod. "This house is haunted."

"No, not haunted," Molly corrected. *"If it were, you would be running out*

screaming. We are not harmful ghosts. We love our mortal family."

Autumn looked around the room. "You said 'we'. As in more than one. There are more ghosts?"

"Molly and her parents live here with us," I explained. "They are actually our relatives. It's a long story that I'll tell you later. For now, just know they are not a threat. It's actually quite nice having Molly around. I hope you'll give her a chance and get to know her."

"But can we—" Halting midsentence, Autumn looked at me.

I knew what she wanted to ask. "Maybe we should keep Molly's existence to ourselves for now. My parents are planning a big open house soon, and they plan to introduce the Greyson's to the entire town then. We just want everyone to know the truth about them. They are harmless entities trying to co-exist in our world."

The evening went smoothly after the initial shock of inviting a ghost to a slumber party. Autumn and Emma had question after question for Molly, once they had adjusted to her presence. Molly seemed quite pleased to answer all their questions.

I was just happy that we could all be friends.

It was hard to believe I had been in school for two weeks. What was even harder to believe was I actually liked my new school and my classes. I saw Dillon at lunch and every evening he wasn't practicing with the basketball team. My best friends, Autumn and Emma spent afternoons with me at my house, doing homework and studying for up-coming tests. Of course, they also enjoyed having Molly around, and Molly was thrilled to have friends. As far as I could tell, they had not shared our little secret with anyone.

Dad had designed a magnificent layout for our backyard. He hired an elite crew to come build a humongous backyard barbeque pit, while Mom knocked herself out designing the furniture to go with it. In a matter of two short weeks they had turned our rather dull backyard area into party central. They had decided to invite all their new friends for an Open House Barbeque. What better weekend to do that but Labor Day? I also invited my new friends from school. With the RSVP's I received, it looked like the entire school would be there. Everyone was excited to meet the Greyson's. Well, everyone except Kenzie, who said 'maybe' she would attend.

Mom put up posters at all of the local businesses to announce the backyard party. The kids at school called it the 'Soiree of Summer', whatever that meant. I knew Mom and Dad wanted to welcome everyone into their new home, but they also had an ulterior motive. They were going to introduce the Greyson's to the town.

Would the townspeople embrace their ghostly neighbors or fear them?

* * *

LABOR Day finally arrived.

Tilly and Mom had been making *hors d'oeuvres* for several days and filling our fridge. Mrs. Greyson spent her time watching and talking to them as they worked.

Amazingly, Dad and Mr. Greyson had become great friends. Dad would discuss new building projects with him and they would trouble shoot the problems together. It was shaping up to be very beneficial for the company.

When Dad announced that Mr. Clemets, the CEO of Indie Architecture, Inc., would be attending the party Mom went berserk cleaning. I helped when I could, but with school I had my hands full.

People started arriving about four o'clock, an hour earlier than the invitation had announced. It seemed the entire town was abuzz with being able to tour the Kotter Estate after it had been vacant for so many years. The barbeque was an added plus.

Dillon and Molly were in my room, watching the cars crowd up the driveway, while I finished getting ready for the party. I noticed Molly seemed a bit apprehensive.

"That's a lot of people," Molly said. *"What if they are frightened of us?"*

"Some might be," Dillon admitted with a shrug. "But remember, your parents and all of us will be here with you. It'll be a piece of cake."

"Dillon's right," I said. "Be your usual sweet self and everyone will love you. Just keep the ice crystals and cold air to a minimum."

I laughed and Molly laughed along with me.

When I was finally ready, we went down to greet Clay and Autumn.

The next thing I knew Autumn had dragged me into the library, leaving Dillon and Clay standing there looking bewildered. Emma burst into the room. Autumn threw out her hand to show us an enormous ring on her finger.

"Clay gave me his class ring," Autumn blurted out between giggles. "Can you believe it? Isn't it just gorgeous? And tonight I'll get to wear his letterman's jacket when it gets cold."

"Um, it's great," I said. "But aren't they both a little large for you?"

"What?" Autumn waved her hand with the heavy ring. "No, it means we're going steady. I'm officially his girlfriend."

"Oh," I said, feeling a little out of step with the local social rules.

Emma looked puzzled. "How did you go steady in California?"

"We didn't 'go steady'," I explained. "It was just an understanding that when you dated you were a couple."

For a moment I pictured myself wearing Dillon's class ring and letterman's jacket.

"Earth to Molly," Autumn called. "I asked you if you are ready to go outside."

Blinking my way back to the present, I nodded. "Yes. Let's go."

A long black limousine pulled up, just as we walked onto the front porch. Dad rushed past us to meet the car. It must be Mr. Clemets. Who else would arrive so elegantly? Dad had been so thrilled when the RSVP came from Mr. Clemets. He had never met the man, yet he was Dad's employer. Mom stood next to me, allowing Dad to do the honors of welcoming his employer.

The chauffer opened the door. Out stepped a tall man with silvery grey hair. Dressed in crisp khakis and a yellow long-sleeved shirt, he looked like he had just walked off a golf course. However, he was very pale, like someone who spent a lot of time inside behind a desk.

Dad reached out his hand, but Mr. Clemets didn't return the offer. Instead he nodded and smiled. It seemed odd to me, but Dad didn't appear offended. He escorted Mr. Clemets to where we were standing.

As Dad made the introductions, I studied Mr. Clemets. Something was off about him. I couldn't put my finger on it, but I had that weird feeling in my gut.

Dillon reached out his hand when he was introduced, but once again Mr. Clemets just nodded and smiled, not taking the hand.

Okay, was this guy germ-a-phobic or just plain rude?

Dad led Mr. Clemets under the tent and seated him in the front row.

I was surprised to see so many kids from school. I even spotted Kenzie scuttling through the crowd. I recognized many of the town business owners here with their families. Even Mrs. Hill was here with the guard that had escorted us into the Town Hall archives. They looked pretty friendly and were even holding hands.

As the sun began to dip toward the tops of the large oak trees lining the drive, heralding sunset, Dad motioned to me.

On cue I went over and rang the large dinner bell that hung from an oak post. It was one of the antiques left on the property Mom had insisted on keeping. She said it added charm to the place.

When everyone heard the bell, they began to gather on the front lawn. Once the majority of the crowd was assembled, my dad came to the front of the porch.

"Welcome to my home," Dad said in a strong voice that needed no assistance from a microphone. "I am so very pleased that you could all attend our first of hopefully many backyard barbeques."

The crowd whistled and applauded.

"Many of you who have lived in Kottersville for a while know this as the Kotter Estate," he continued. "Recently we discovered valuable information concerning this property. Records state that it was originally owned by William Greyson. No, not me, but my great-grandfather. It has also been confirmed that the estate was originally built by the Greyson Architectural and Construction Company owned by William Greyson in 1876. Today I am officially announcing that this will now be known as the Greyson Estate."

More applause rumbled across the lawn.

Mr. Clemets walked up next to Dad and whispered in his ear. I saw Dad nod and he backed away, giving Mr. Clemets the opportunity to speak.

"My name is Mr. Clemets. I am CEO of Indie Architecture, Inc. I am honored to be here on such a beautiful fall day. The restoration to the estate is remarkable, and we are quite fortunate to have the Greyson family reside here once again. As of this moment, I am stepping down from my CEO position and appointing Mr. William Greyson to replace me as the new CEO. I am also reinstating the name of Greyson Architectural and Construction Company, the original name of my company. He and his family will be based here in hopes of opening up many business opportunities for all of you. Thank you."

Mr. Clemets ended his speech with a wave and backed away, returning the crowd to Dad.

"I'm honored and very taken by surprise," Dad said, his voice quivering. "Thank you, Mr. Clemets, for the opportunity. And for restoring the original name of the company."

"If I may," the Town Manager said, coming forward. "I'd like to say something as well."

Two other men with bulging muscles followed behind him carrying a large board covered with billowing material. They stood the board on the ground at the foot of the porch steps and then faced the crowd.

"I have recently learned that over the years your company and your family played a huge part in the forming of our community," the Town Manager continued. "It has also been called to my attention that records in our own Town Hall archives show that some underhanded dealings took place over a hundred years ago. The town name was changed when Benjamin Kotter took over as Town Commissioner in 1886. The original name for our fair city was Greysontown."

A wave of gasps echoed through the crowd.

"Today," he continued, "we are proud to turn a wrong into a right. By a unanimous decision of the Town Board we are reinstating the original town name and making it official with this new city limits sign."

He motioned to the men. The two burly men pulled the silky material off the board revealing the new sign. It read:

Welcome to Greysontown, Indiana
Population: 5,438

After a little quick math, I realized the new number included us.

Dad beamed from ear to ear. Mom began to cry. I was speechless. The crowd roared with approval.

Dillon picked me up in his arms and twirled me around.

But Dad had one more announcement.

Dad cleared his throat to get the attention of the crowd.

The chatter stopped, and all eyes turned to him.

"I am nearly speechless," Dad admitted. "I'm certain if you asked my wife and daughter they would say that my being speechless is a rare occasion. But I have another announcement." Dad cleared his throat. "I have heard from Charlie my barber, Martha at the local flower shop, and even Hector the head chef at my favorite restaurant here in town, just to name a few, that the Kotter Estate is rumored to be haunted. I am here today to clarify all the rumors."

Dad paused and moved slightly to the right to expose a full view of the entrance to the house.

"Some of you may not believe in ghosts," he continued. "I never really considered it one way or the other. But I stand here today to tell you I am now a firm believer. Ghosts do exist."

The crowd stilled. No murmurs. No shuffling feet. The only sound was insects trilling in the distance.

"To those of you who might still be skeptical or think I have lost my mind, I would like to introduce you to William and Laura Greyson and their daughter, Molly."

Dad stepped even further out of the way and the Greyson's along with Molly appeared in the doorway just inside the entrance.

Gasps rolled through the crowd. One woman let out a pinched scream and stumbled backward.

However, I noticed there was a smile on Mr. Clemets face.

"This is a hoax," said one man in the crowd. "A hologram designed to make this a night to remember. I say we go inside and meet these ghosts and see for ourselves."

Then several more men shouted in agreement.

"Greyson, this is outstanding," another man said. "I love that you have embraced the whole haunted estate idea and made such a spectacular effort to entertain us."

The crowd began to line up to enter the house and meet the so-called holograms.

Dillon and I quickly stepped inside ahead of the crowd.

"Molly, I'll stand here with you," I reassured her. "Don't be afraid. They're more afraid of you than you are of them. Trust me."

Dad, Mom, and Mrs. Darby stood with us, as the people began filing through the front door. The Greyson's and Molly hovered just above the floor between all of us. The first couple waved their hands at the Greyson's forms and found them to be icy cold as small crystals formed on their hands.

"How are you doing this, Greyson?" one man asked. "Marvelous!"

"I can't take credit for it," Dad replied. "They are really here. William and Laura are my great-grandparents."

The couple stepped back and studied the figures in front of them. The crowd pressed to get inside, filling up the living area. They overflowed onto the staircase to see above the rest who had crowded around the three figures.

"Can you make them do something to convince us they are real?" someone shouted.

Dad looked at William for help.

With a nod, William and Laura floated high into the air and stared down at the crowd. Molly stayed close to me.

"Yeah, that's a good trick," the same guy said. "But can you make them talk?"

William floated over to the man, who was immediately drenched in a fog of cold air. *What would you like for me to say, Sir? I am what I am, simply a ghost. But if you need more persuading I will accommodate you.*

William began to spin so fast he became a blur. Ice crystals showered down on the crowd, landing in hair and on clothing. Then he stopped.

"Are you still skeptical?"

"I don't think Greyson is trying to pull anything over on us," the man said, his voice cracking into a high pitch. "These—these are the real deal. Greyson Estate is haunted!"

A hush came over the people stuffed into the area encircling the Greyson's. The circle began to expand, pushing others out the door.

"Wait!" Dad called, as people began to shove one another to get out the door. "The Greyson's are not hostile. They are kind and friendly. Please stay and meet them. If you do, I think you will agree that ghosts and humans can coexist. Please, give them a chance."

The crowd halted and began turning around. Once again they formed an orderly line and William floated back to his wife's side.

As the people filed through there were cordial hellos and a few still skeptical stares as they passed the Greyson's. William and Laura were gracious and answered any questions people had as they passed by.

After about an hour, the last group of people finished their tour of the house and went to the backyard where the food was being served. A beautiful waxing crescent moon hung over the field beyond the yard.

Dillon and I had gotten all the fire pits started and the fire felt wonderful in the chilly night air. Then across the yard next to the barn I noticed something that reflected the light of the fire as it danced in the pit. I strained to see what it was as the heat from the flame gave a quivering impression. I walked around the fire pit and toward the barn.

"Where are you going, Molly?' Dillon asked, following me.

"I need to see what is catching the reflection of the fire," I said, continuing to walk toward the darkness.

Then, I stopped dead in my tracks.

"No, no, no, no!" I shouted.

Dillon stopped beside me. "Is that what I think it is?" he asked in a whisper.

I couldn't form an answer. There sat a red box with glass windows with a carnival Gypsy inside it. I moved closer, stopping about a foot from the machine. It was the same Gypsy with the pealing face and faded paisley dress and missing little finger on her right hand.

Turning to Dillon, I held out my hand. With a sigh, he pulled a dollar bill from his wallet and placed it in my hand. I waited until he placed a second dollar bill on top of the first one. By now I knew the routine.

With a deep breath, I leaned down and put the first bill into the slot. The Gypsy began to move slowly, as if waking up from a mechanical nap. I placed the second bill in the slot and waited. I stared into her dark eyes. It was as if we knew each other intimately.

A card popped out of the other slot and landed next to my feet. I reached for it, but another hand scooped it up first.

I looked up and saw Mr. Clemets.

"I see you have found my Gypsy once again," he said.

His Gypsy?

"How do you know I have seen this Gypsy before?" I asked.

"Let's go inside and I'll explain," he said still holding the card.

Dillon held my hand, as we followed Mr. Clemets into the house.

Once inside, I stopped in the kitchen and refused to move any further. "Tell me what you have to do with the Gypsy."

"Please indulge me a bit further," Mr. Clemets implored. "May we go a little further out of ear shot?"

With a shrug, I led him into the living area. There Dillon and I sat on the couch.

"I owe you an explanation," Mr. Clemets said.

"Darn right you owe me an explanation," I replied in a rather sharp voice. "Cough it up."

"Please, hear me out," Mr. Clemets requested. "Getting your father here was easy, but I knew he wouldn't be an easy sell on the idea of ghosts. That is why I turned my attention to you. Young people these days are so interested in the supernatural. I needed to get you to believe in ghosts, so that when you met the ones here you would accept them."

"Okay, hold on," I said, waving my hands. "You mean you knew there were ghosts in this house before we moved here?"

"Most certainly," Mr. Clemets answered, calm and unruffled.

"But what does the Gypsy have to do with it all?" I asked.

"I simply used the Gypsy as a means to plant the idea of ghosts in your head," he replied. "I believe the cards were most helpful."

"But I just happened to see her out front of our hotel in Las Vegas," I argued.

"Not exactly. I took a risk placing the Gypsy in front of your hotel in hopes you would do the rest on your own. And you did, quite nicely I must say. The first card you received was planted there by me for you." Mr. Clemets paused to give a quiet laugh. "My, you wouldn't believe how many people I had to steer away from that Gypsy, before you spotted her and came out to investigate."

"This is not funny," I snapped. "That Gypsy really freaked me out. Especially when I saw her at the gas station. And again at the carnival. Should I even ask how you did that?"

Mr. Clemets gave a casual shrug and looked quite pleased with himself. "I gave your father specific instructions on where to gas up the vehicle for the journey east. That made it easy for you to run into the Gypsy another time before leaving Las Vegas. Here in Indiana I knew your new friends would not allow you to miss the biggest event of the summer, the carnival. Yes, it all came together quite nicely. You were an excellent participant."

"You put a lot of work into something that could've gone really wrong if I hadn't been so gullible," I grumbled, sinking back into the couch cushions.

"Ah, yes," Mr. Clemets replied. "But you were very curious. It led you to the exact place I had intended, the town archives."

"Why the archives?" I asked, thoroughly confused. "What could you possibly want me to find? There was nothing there that had anything to do with you."

"Wait," Dillon said, jumping into the conversation. "You were using Molly as a way to gain information about the house and the Greyson's? What are you, some kind of con artist? Maybe Molly's dad would be interested to know how you used his daughter to gain information."

Dillon stood up to leave, but the Greyson's and Molly entered the room.

"We heard your voices in here," Mr. Greyson said. *"I hope you don't mind if we join you."*

Then William saw Mr. Clemets and immediately floated over to him. He studied him closely, making a complete circle around him. I wasn't certain if he was going to dump an avalanche of ice on him in anger or worse.

"Father, is it really you?" Mr. Greyson asked. "Clemet Greyson?"

My mouth dropped open and a small whimper escaped.

"I have missed you, William," Mr. Clemets said, smiling at his son. "Laura, it is so good to see you again. And, Molly you are as beautiful as the day you turned sixteen. It is wonderful that everyone is back home and together where they belong."

"You are Mr. Greyson's father?" I asked, struggling to keep my composure. "But how can that be? If it's true, then you have to be a— ghost."

Just as I said that, he reached for my hand. His touch was icy cold just like Molly's touch. Small crystals formed on my hand. I looked down at my hand and believed.

"But you go out in public," I said. "You're CEO of an international company. Ghosts just don't do that."

"I have been a ghost for a great length of time, my dear," Mr. Clements replied. "I have learned many 'tricks' to expand my existence and allow me to walk among the living. I do not stay outside for very long, nor do I touch anyone I do not want to know my secret. I also have spent decades communicating with the living through the telephone and before that I used the telegraph system. There have only been a small number of people who have seen me face to face."

"You needed me to acquire the information in order to get the house back into my family's hands," I said. "You also needed us to do the physical work to bring the Greyson's back to this house and reunite them with Molly. I was the family piece you needed without sending up red flags on your keen interest." I paused, considering the facts. "Why didn't you just expose Benjamin Kotter yourself?"

"Because, my dear Molly," Mr. Clemets answered, "I technically do not exist. I cannot explain it to you. I watched painfully for years as I stood by educating myself on the trickery of being a ghost. While all this took place I could not intercede. Just understand that I am deeply appreciative for your cooperation in helping find the answers to save your family heritage. You, my dear, are the one who brought all this out in the open for me—for our family. You are strong and have a good heart, Molly Greyson the second."

"That's another thing that has me confused. How was it that my family names are so like the Greyson's family names?" I asked, hoping he had a rational answer.

"Fate, my dear." Mr. Clemets smiled and turned toward William. "It is time I must leave you now. My business is complete. I go with peace in my heart and wait for another time in which we will meet again."

Mr. Clemets, or rather Mr. Greyson, hovered for a moment, smiling down at us. Then in a cloud of vapor, he disappeared through the back door and up into the night sky.

A piece of paper floated like a feather to the floor. I recognized it as the card Clemet had picked up from the Gypsy.

I grabbed the card and silently read the words printed on it: *Thank you, Molly Greyson, from your great-great-great-grandfather.*

CHAPTER 27

THE rest of the evening played out like a dream.

The Greyson's, Dillon, and I swore that we'd keep the meeting with Clemet Greyson a secret. Clemet had officially turned the company over to Dad and had graciously bowed out of the business. It was as if he had been waiting for decades to find the rightful heir. I believed he had left this world in peace.

William was grateful to have seen his father again. I was still miffed about being maneuvered into working for a ghost, but it had all worked out for the best. Since I came from a long line of entrepreneurs, maybe their savvy business genes had carried over to me and I'd be head of the company one day.

Dillon and I joined the rest of the kids from school that were still hanging out around the fire pit. They were laughing and hi-fiving each other for having become friends with real ghosts.

The chill in the air had turned it into an early fall night, and I wished I had thought to grab my sweater before coming outside. I wasn't used to the seasons changing so rapidly. It would be a nice change, though, from the constant sun and hot weather.

Autumn looked cozy warm wrapped in Clay's letterman's jacket.

Emma and Bryan looked like they were having a good time. I strained to see if Emma was wearing Bryan's class ring but from where I was sitting I couldn't tell.

Then I saw Kenzie. She was sitting all alone next to the fire. I had to admit that I felt a slight bit of pity for her. Maybe I shouldn't have run the old Dylan off so soon. They would have made such a great couple.

"What are we going to do with the Gypsy?" Dillon asked, pointing toward the barn.

I looked over and saw the Gypsy alone in the red box with its glass windows. For some reason she didn't look as foreboding. I actually felt rather sorry for her.

"I think I'll keep her," I said with a nod. "She's become a big part of why we are here. It might be hard to explain to Dad, although Mom will love her antique quality. I'll just say she was a gift from Mr. Clemets.

Which is true, just not the whole truth."

"A lot has happened in the month you have been in Indiana, Molly," Dillon said. "I really don't want to complicate things, but I need to do this before I lose my courage." He stood up in front of me. "Hold out your hand."

"Why? What's wrong with my hand?" I held out my left hand, turning it over and back again.

With a smile, he turned my hand palm down. He pulled his class ring off his finger and placed it on mine. It was heavy and much too large. Fire reflected off the giant purple stone.

"One more thing," Dillon said.

He reached for something behind the chair. It was his letterman's jacket. He placed it around my shoulders and helped me slip my arms inside the sleeves. The warmth was welcoming.

I glanced down at cuffs that hung to my knees. I probably looked ridiculous, but I had never had anything fit me as well as that jacket. It felt wonderful.

I wrapped my arms around Dillon's waist, the overlong sleeves flopping, and gave him a tight hug. He returned the affection and added a kiss to make it official.

Looking over Dillon's shoulder, I saw Molly standing in the ballroom window. She was smiling down at us.

I had never been happier in my life.

All thanks to a house in Greysontown, Indiana.

THE END

About the Author

Roberta Hoffer is a retired preschool teacher from a small town in Indiana. She has been married to her high school sweetheart, Kevin, for forty-seven years. They raised two children, Amy and Andrew, and have one grandson, Christian.

Roberta loves animals and is an advocate for animal rights. She owns two Yorkshire Terriers, Minnie and Buddy, both rescues. When not writing she enjoys doing family outings such as paddle boarding, zip lining, climbing mountains, and exercise walking. Her ultimate passion has always been writing books for children that will give back the joy they gave her when teaching.

Awards include the 2014 National Purple Dragonfly Award for first place in children's literacy for children's chapter books for "The Ghost of Stonebridge Lane" *(Book I of The Stonebridge Ghost Tales)*. "The Ghost of the Frozen North" *(Book II of The Stonebridge Ghost Tales)* won the 2015 National Purple Dragonfly Award for second place in children's literacy for children's chapter books. *The Stonebridge Ghost Tales* series won the silver medal winner of the Moonbeam Children's Book Awards for 2015 for Best Children's Chapter Book Series.

Ms. Hoffer explains her writing in these words: "I am blessed to be able to write books that I can be proud of and know they can be read by any one regardless of age while conveying Christian values." Her personal advice to everyone is to treat people the way you would like to be treated and to always put God first in your life.

* * * * *

Publications

Publications by Roberta Hoffer include the following:

Young Adult Novels:
Molly Greyson's Ghost
The Cubicle Detective

* * *

The Stonebridge Ghost Tales
Juvenile Fantasy series (in order):
The Ghost of Stonebridge Lane
The Ghost of the Frozen North
The Ghosts of Stony Manor

* * *

Children's Picture Books:
Minnie to the Rescue
Nakita's Big Question

* * * * *